SEA CHANGE

SEA CHANGE

SYLVIA HEHIR

STONE COLD FOX PRESS

Winner of the Pitlochry Prize 2018

Published by Stone Cold Fox Press,
an imprint of Stirling Publishing
10 Davidson House
57 Queen Charlotte Street
Edinburgh
EH6 7EY

www.stirlingpublishing.co.uk

CONTENTS

ACKNOWLEDGEMENTS

I am grateful to Tabatha at Stirling Publishing for having belief in this story and for her passion and enthusiasm in bringing it over the finishing line.

For their continuing encouragement and support, I am indebted to all the staff at Scottish Book Trust. Receiving the New Writers Award provided me with a much-needed endorsement, allowing me to work on the early ideas in the book supported by my indispensable and unwavering mentor, Lindsey Fraser.

Massive thanks are due to the many people who helped shape the various drafts, especially members of the DFA workshop, my two supervisors Dr. Elizabeth Reeder and Dr. Rob Maslen, and Dr. Zoë Strachan and Professor Louise Welsh at University of Glasgow.

Attending writing courses at Arvon Centres and at Moniack Mhor provided me with incredible feedback from top-flight authors. Thanks so much to you all. Also, many thanks to the superstar author Claire McFall who awarded *Sea Change* the Scottish Association of Writers Pitlochry Quaich in 2018 and to Keith Gray for his ongoing support.

This is a work of fiction and any misrepresentation of procedures conducted by police officers in real-life situations are entirely due to my own errors. Many thanks to Angie Campbell for talking through the crime related elements of the story.

Chiefly, I couldn't have written this book without the love and encouragement of my family and friends. Thank you, all.

SATURDAY

CHAPTER 1

Alex backed away from the spitting flames and watched Chuck wrench another rotten timber from the cottage doorway, bringing with it an avalanche of plaster and brickwork.

'Give us a hand,' Chuck called.

Alex sprinted the short distance to the derelict Keeper's Cottage, his bare feet kicking up soft sand as he went. But Daniel stayed where he was, balancing on a floorboard they'd ripped from the cottage kitchen, its nails still poking through.

It had taken the three of them all afternoon—positioning boulders in a circle on the sand for the fire pit, scouring the oak woodlands behind the cottage to collect a mound of wood, ransacking the innards of the cottage itself. They'd had no fear of being disturbed; the only visitors to this part of the peninsula were the deer—until Chuck had set up camp, that is.

With a breeze from the sea, the lads' shorts flapped against their legs. Daniel wore his AC/DC t-shirt, but the other two were bare-chested. The evening was warm, even without the heat from the fire.

Chuck took a large beam in both hands and hurled it into the flames, causing an explosion of sparks to spume into the evening sky. The cracked windowpanes of the Keeper's Cottage blinked back the fiery glare. When he considered the time was right Chuck used a long stick to rake the embers, then he signalled to Alex to help position the floorboard, carefully placing each end on granite blocks so that it was suspended a few centimetres above the flattened bed of flickering coals.

Chuck tugged at the waist-cord of his tribal-patterned shorts and let them pool at his feet. Naked now, he gave a bow to Alex and a curtsy to Daniel.

Turning to the fire, he slid his left foot onto the floorboard then, taking his time, tiptoed along. As he approached the centre of the ring of fire he bounced lightly on his toes but the wood remained solid beneath him despite the smoke pluming off its underside.

He pirouetted to face the two friends. Carefully placing one foot behind the other, he walked backwards, smiling widely as he went, then stopped a few centimetres short of the end of the plank. He executed a perfect back flip and landed on the mat of bracken they'd positioned earlier. He raised his arms in the air like the athlete he was, leg muscles taut, skin gleaming with sweat.

The performance over, he strutted around the fire towards Daniel and Alex, his hand held out, seeking the approbation he knew he deserved.

Chuck quickly pulled on his shorts, gave Alex a playful kick up the bum with his bare foot and said, 'Your turn.'

TUESDAY

CHAPTER 2

Alex came to a halt when he reached the cliff edge. He could see his wooden boat pitching about on the stormy waters below, straining at its painter.

Daniel was limping along the clifftop path behind him. 'I'll only be a few minutes,' Alex called.

'We'll be late,' Daniel yelled back against the wind. Alex knew full well that Daniel freaked at being late for anything. The first day back at school was a big deal for him.

Alex stared again at the crashing waves. Last night's storm had made a fitting end to the summer holidays. He really needed to haul his boat back to the safety of the sheltered beach before she suffered any damage. Decision made, he grabbed a handful of heather and scrambled over the cliff edge. The worn soles of his trainers skidded on the rain-drenched rocky slope as he skewed his way down to the cove.

His cheap trainers were just as useless on the piles of seaweed dumped at the foot of the cliffs by the storm. With his eyes fixed on his boat, he'd only taken a few stumbling steps when he lurched over a stinking heap and fell face down. Swearing loudly, he pulled himself onto his knees and winced with pain as he wiped blood from a wound where his forehead had hit a rock. On his feet now, Alex swore again as he aimed a kick at the mound he'd tripped over. But he stopped mid-kick—seized by the sight of two pale fingers poking out from the seaweed.

There was no mistaking what lay amid the tangled bladderwrack and kelp.

Alex stared at the body, at the jean-clad legs, stiff in their unnatural position, only turning away when he heard Daniel's voice tearing through the wind like the demanding call of a fledgling seagull: 'Hurry up.'

Alex could see him peering over the cliff edge, his hands shielding his eyes from the morning sun.

'I'm coming,' Alex yelled back. 'You wait there.'

But Alex couldn't leave. Living on a croft, Alex was no stranger to putrid finds. Yet this was no unfortunate beast. This was—had been—a person. A teenager, judging by the clothes. He tugged at a frond of leathery kelp that lay across the head and a haze of black flies lifted off. Alex had barely enough time to step away when he saw the exposed mangled flesh where the face should have been. He retched out a stream of bitter-tasting liquid.

Now he'd seen enough.

Pebbles skittered down the cliff face. Daniel, beyond anxious, was navigating the slope.

Alex backed away from the mound where the flies were already beginning to settle again and yelled up to Daniel. 'Stay where you are.'

He patted his phone in his pocket. No signal down here. Phoning the police would have to wait until he got closer to the village.

'What is it?'

'Just stay there.' There was no need for Daniel to witness this.

Alex gave a last scan up and down the body, and froze, his attention caught by a patch of white on the navy jumper the body was wearing. Blocking his nostrils with his hand, he squatted to get a better look. A small white anchor was embroidered on the cuff.

Alex knew there was only one jumper in the world like that—knew because Aunty Joan had knitted it for him last Christmas. It was the jumper Alex had joked he'd never be seen dead in. The one he'd lent to Chuck after a late-night swim.

What the ...? A mix of emotions churned in his gut. He kicked out again at the pile of stinking seaweed. After all that had gone on—it couldn't end like this.

Alex turned and staggered towards the cliff. 'I said ... stay there,' he shouted to Daniel, unable to keep the panic out of his voice.

'We'll be late,' Daniel called from his perch.

'You go back.'

Alex began a double-quick ascent of the rocks, knowing through familiarity the best hand and footholds.

9

'I think I'm stuck,' Daniel said, shuffling his feet. The loosened soil hit Alex in the face. 'It's quarter to nine. And my leg...'

'I know. I know. I'm behind you.' Alex pulled himself to within an arm's length of Daniel. 'Just go back.'

They climbed to the sound of Daniel's grunts until they reached the grasses on the open clifftop, both of them red in the face.

Daniel stooped over, his hands gripping his thighs. 'What is it? What did you find down there?'

'It's ... nothing.'

'Cut the crap. You look dreadful. What happened to your face?'

Alex took a deep breath, placed the tips of his fingers against the lump that was growing on his forehead.

'For God's sake, Alex. What's happened?'

Alex shrugged his shoulders. Shook his head. What words could he use? There were no words. But Daniel started to limp towards the cliff edge.

'No. Don't!'

'What is it? Tell me.'

'On the ... beach ...'

'What? Another sick game arranged by Chuck?' Daniel sneered and brushed his hair off his face.

'You ... You don't know what you're saying.'

Daniel's face was turning an angry red. 'Well why don't you just tell me!'

All right. If Daniel reckoned he wanted to know: 'It *is* Chuck. In the seaweed.'

'What do you mean "in the seaweed"?' A look of horror fixed on Daniel's face as realisation struck him. 'Chuck's *body*, do you mean?'

Alex gave a brief nod.

'You mean ... Chuck's dead?'

Yes, Chuck was dead. Chuck, who had more life in his little finger nail than all the kids in school put together.

The boys stared at each other as the wind howled around them.

Daniel shivered in his white school shirt. 'What the ...? How?'

Alex gave a shrug.

'Was it a fire?'

Alex closed his eyes; saw again the body, the clothes, the ragged flesh. Whatever had happened, Chuck hadn't got caught in any fire. 'No. Not that,' he said.

It was Daniel's voice that shook with panic now. 'Do you reckon he was found?'

Had Chuck been found? Had the blokes that Chuck had obviously been so scared of found his hiding place?

'I don't know, do I? All I know is that he's down there. Or at least what's left of him.' Alex turned his back to the sea. 'I've never seen ... never seen anyone ... you know?'

Daniel hunched his shoulders, wrapped his arms around his chest. 'Chuck's dead.'

Alex took a step closer to Daniel. His shivering had turned into full-blown quaking. 'It'll be all right.'

'Yeah.' Daniel slipped his backpack off his shoulder. 'I'll call the police.' He stuck a shaking hand into his bag.

'No signal here,' Alex said.

'But emergency numbers—'

'No. Really ... Wait.'

Daniel had his phone in his hand. 'What for?' He frowned. 'What is it?'

Alex grabbed both of Daniel's arms. 'Just let me think, will you? ... Nobody's seen us here,' Alex said. 'The tide's almost at its lowest point. I'll think of something.' He puffed out his cheeks before releasing a deep breath. 'We need to get to school.'

'Fucksake, Alex. We can't just leave him there. We've got to do—'

'We've got to do what? What're you saying?'

Daniel shook Alex's hands off. 'We have to tell the police.' His voice had regained a level of composure.

'Look at it like this.' Alex paused and fixed his eyes on Daniel's. 'He's not going anywhere until the next high tide at the earliest ... It doesn't have to be us.'

'What do you mean?'

'There's no need for us to freak out ... Draw attention to ourselves. Somebody else will find him soon enough.'

'It doesn't have to be us?' Daniel didn't sound convinced.

'It'll be better all round if we keep out of it. Agreed?'

'How can we?'

'Look, we've done nothing wrong.'

Daniel lifted his eyebrows.

'Well, *you've* done nothing wrong.' Alex said. 'Chuck's not spoken to anybody else since he came here. No one knows anything about him.'

Daniel jabbed his finger towards the cove. 'You're not seriously suggesting we ignore the fact that you've just found ...? That Chuck is ...'

Alex stepped towards the clifftop. Above him, a pair of terns wheeled chaotically—white, black, white against the bleached blue sky. All of this was so wrong. 'You know I can't let my mum find out anything,' he said eventually. 'We've got to keep quiet. Can I trust you to do that?'

'But we can't—' Daniel said flatly, the fight having gone out of him.

'We can. Give me until the end of the day.'

'That's too long. What if—'

'I'll sort it. Really.'

Daniel checked the time on his mobile. Not bothering to hide his reluctance, he set off down the path, leaning into the wind.

'And they probably won't even give you your timetable, dressed like that,' Daniel pointed out as they neared the school gates.

Alex shrugged. Unlike Daniel, who had new clothes bought for him at the start of every new school year, Alex owned none of the items of the dress code the Depute demanded they adhere to, even in their fifth year. School uniform was definitely lower down the priority list than chicken feed at the croft.

'See you in English then? And … you won't do anything stupid?'

Alex shrugged again, preoccupied by his thoughts. 'Aye. I'll see you …'

They'd been friends since primary school—Alex and Daniel, two names that were always said together—but English was the only subject they'd be in together now that Daniel was starting his Highers. It was the one school subject Alex found easy. The rest of the time he'd be doing 'Skills for Work' subjects. Some joke! He regularly told anybody who would listen that being a fisherman was the only work he wanted to do. And he was already better skilled at that than any of the so-called tutors.

He hadn't a clue when the English class was but Alex already knew he wouldn't be in classes that day, and it had nothing to do with his lack of uniform.

Alex waited until Daniel had merged with the other swotty fifth-years entering the science wing, then leaned against the redbrick wall near the smokers getting their last fix before morning break. He knew what he had to do.

At the first bell, the smokers strolled off towards the main entrance, a couple of them nodding to him as they passed by. Then when the late bell rang and there were no more stragglers to be seen, Alex skirted along the building to retrace his steps to the clifftop, already planning how to fix things. Trust Chuck to choose that spot to turn up dead. The very place where they'd first met. The few weeks since that day had turned in to a living nightmare. Alex would make sure that it all ended—here and now.

As he strode across the headland, he looked out to sea to check he wouldn't be spotted from any nearby crafts. The fishing boats that had left the harbour at dawn were now just dots in the distance. He could make out the CalMac ferry edging along the horizon, heading to the Outer Isles. All safe enough. The cove was difficult to get to and the morning dog-walkers preferred the long beach. He could do it.

He knew what he needed: lengths of rope, pieces of netting, at least two large rocks. He almost gave up on the plan at the thought of tying the rope around the stinking body. He had to get a grip, prepare himself for what had to be done. He thought through how he would have to drag the body into the sea, tying it to the towrope then rowing out past the headland. And how he would need to tie the rocks, wrapped in the netting, to the body's turgid limbs before tipping the rocks overboard. He vowed he would stay watching until the skull with its gaping eye sockets and ragged flesh sank beneath the waves. That would be the last he'd see of Chuck, his pale hand giving a final salute, taking with him the white anchor on the jumper. Well, Alex wouldn't be waving back.

Alex stopped. The anchor on the cuff! With the realisation that he didn't have to dispose of the body, he very nearly laughed out loud. All he needed to do was cut the anchor off the jumper. It was just another navy jumper then. Nobody would be able to link it back to him. Nobody else knew what had gone on during the summer.

Alex balanced on the cliff edge. The tide, now at its lowest point, had exposed the sandy reaches that linked his cove to the long beach. Out at the tide line, a woman wearing black wellies stood watching the waves crash in. It was Mrs MacKinnon. And Scamp, her frisky spaniel, was chasing up the beach towards the piles of seaweed.

CHAPTER 3

Alex staggered back, clamping his lips together to squash the howl that wanted to escape, determined to fight his rising panic. He crouched beside a gorse bush and gulped in a deep breath. Took another, deeper breath, this time holding it in his lungs for a count of five before letting it go. He stayed there, folded up, concentrating on his breathing, until enough time had passed for Mrs MacKinnon to follow Scamp up the beach and make her discoveries.

A hooded crow landed close to him and started strutting through the windblown grasses. Alex had hated hooded crows ever since he'd come across one up the hill, pecking out the warm innards from a stillborn lamb. He jumped up and waved his arms around. The crow hopped a few metres away, closer to the cliff edge. Alex searched around for a stone to throw but the crow took off and flew to a nearby birch tree, the branch it landed on flexing against the sudden weight.

Alex paced back to his spot on the cliff edge. Mrs MacKinnon had gone—rushing into the village with her news, without doubt. Before long, his cove would become a circus. And Chuck, still sporting the jumper with its white anchor, the main attraction.

'Don't do it,' a jokey voice shouted.

Twisting around quickly, Alex saw Moth sauntering towards him along the cliff path.

'How's the craic?' she asked when she reached him.

'Moth! What're you up to?'

Moth scratched the side of her head where black stubble showed through the shaved section of her scalp. Her short, black hair had been sculpted into intricate contours making it look like the paws of a furry monkey clinging to the sides of her head.

'Just going back.' She clanked the bag she was carrying. 'Empties mostly. Sorry,' she said. 'We'd planned a beach party last night ...' She stopped speaking, shook her head to think. 'I texted you about it ... didn't I?'

'You did. But, you know, night before first day back. I didn't want to upset my mum.'

Moth nodded, giving what looked like her best impression of a wise and understanding friend. 'We didn't make it to the beach anyway,' she said. 'Too wet.'

'Too wet! It was almost a hurricane.'

'Missed that,' Moth said, shaking her head.

Alex eyed Moth. 'What're you doing now?'

She thought for a moment. 'Home probably. Unless you've something better on offer.'

Alex ignored her ridiculous come-on. Fucksake. Apart from everything else, they were cousins.

'You might as well help me then,' he said.

She didn't complain when he took the bag of empties from her and stashed it under a nearby bush.

'Come on,' he said, leading her towards a longer but less precipitous descent than the rock face to the cove. This way they would encounter nothing worse than grassy knolls and rocky outcrops ... and would avoid the stinking piles of seaweed.

'So why aren't you there?' Moth asked as she slithered down a sand dune on her bottom.

'What?'

'Why aren't you at school?'

'Long story,' Alex said before he could stop himself.

'Ooh. Goody.'

'No. It's nothing really. I'll go later when I've emptied my creels. I couldn't get the boat out yesterday—you know—Storm Kathleen.' Moth shrugged. 'And I've promised Tony a lobster. If I let him down he'll go to somebody else.'

The sun warmed the air and the salty onshore wind buffeted around them. When they reached the long beach, they took off their trainers to paddle through the shallow waters until they came alongside Alex's boat in the cove. Alex hauled the boat closer and gave her a thorough inspection before letting Moth step in. Then he released the painter, pushed the boat into the slack tide, jumped aboard and took the oars.

Within a few moments, they'd cleared the shelter of the cove and were heading into the swell that lifted the wooden boat as if it were nothing more than an empty hazelnut shell before letting it fall heavily down again.

'Good job I've not had any breakfast,' Moth said.

The sea was quieter when they rounded the headland. Alex eased into a rhythmic pull on the oars and found the strenuous activity helped to curb the panic that still threatened to overwhelm him. Reaching his marker buoy, he engaged the winch that would drag his first creel from the seabed. He'd been eleven when he'd successfully set his first lobster pot. Out fishing with his dad, he baited the creel with mackerel one day and returned the next to find not only a crab but a decent sized lobster too. Dad had given him the money his catch had fetched at the harbour auction and Alex had dutifully started up his savings account under Mum's direction.

Hauling the cumbersome creel over the side of the boat, Alex was grateful for the monotony of the routine. He could work on autopilot: examine the catch and carefully remove any lobster that had crept in; clear out the old bait; then set the creel aside, ready to be re-baited and dropped back into the sea. The blue rubber gloves he'd given Moth to wear were far too big but she quickly learned how to tie the lobster's claws together once he'd measured it up to check the size. He was pleased and surprised at how much help Moth was and they landed his catch in record time.

'I want to look at a few more possible sites while we're out,' he said as Moth, obviously content with her efforts, slumped amid the ropes.

In her nest, Moth nodded an okay before closing her eyes and turning her face to catch the sun's rays.

It was a pull against the wind to get to the part of the peninsula where Chuck had his campsite by the Keeper's Cottage. As they drew closer and closer to the shore there were no obvious signs of recent activity. But Chuck's tent was tucked in the lee of a ravine where a fresh water spring erupted from the crag face.

Alex manoeuvred the boat into a nearby narrow inlet. After nudging Moth's toes to rouse her, he jumped out and pulled the boat onto a strip of sandy beach.

'I won't be long. Will you stay with the boat?'

Moth opened her eyes a fraction to indicate that she'd be fine before wriggling deeper into the pile of ropes.

Viewed from the shore the cottage looked unchanged, despite having had its guts ripped out and burnt.

The circle of boulders that had bordered their fire looked smaller in bright daylight. It was only eight or ten paces across, yet it had seemed like a flickering ocean of flame when Alex had stepped onto the plank. The only remains were a few half-charred sticks fringing the crust of grey ash. The plank had been mostly consumed, but Alex could still make out its straight edges as he tossed pebbles into the centre and watched puffs of ash fly out.

How many times had they each crossed the fire? Chuck daring them, taunting them to take crazier turns. Alex had chickened out at being blindfolded but Daniel had taken it on with a shrug. He'd almost reached the other end, too, before the plank had given way and he'd tumbled into the embers. Alex had screamed at Chuck to help him get Daniel off, but Chuck had said, calmly, 'That's the consequence of taking a risk,' before stalking off to his tent, game over. There was no doubt. Chuck had proved himself to be a complete arsehole.

Alex moved away from the fire pit and crouched on the cottage doorstep. A money spider dropped onto the back of his hand and he let it run over his fingers before flicking it off. A pair of coupling butterflies whirligigged over the nearby sea campion.

Finally, he got up and walked on, beyond the Keeper's Cottage, towards Chuck's tent. Chuck's tent. Ha! For all his fancy gadgets—his iPhone that he couldn't charge and his diver's watch—the tent was nothing but a camouflage tarpaulin thrown over lashed-together branches.

When they'd first met, Alex had assumed Chuck was another wild camper—admittedly more adventurous than the ones who only made it a few hundred metres from the road. He'd even tolerated Chuck's seemingly crazy story of being a runaway. And Alex hadn't minded getting the provisions Chuck had asked for and dropping them at the secluded campsite when he was out fishing anyway.

Chuck's 'kitchen' was still intact: the gas bottle and burner still balanced on the pile of pallets, boxed in with corrugated roofing taken from an outhouse; the fishing rod leaning against a corner. A plastic box, tucked in the crook of the branches of an oak tree, contained an assortment of cutlery and tools. Alex picked out the penknife he'd lent to Chuck when the tin opener had broken. 'Call that a knife? You'd have a job skinning rabbits with that blunt thing,' Chuck had mocked; then he'd shown Alex the hunting knife he kept in his kitbag.

It was a great setup and, for a moment, Alex could see himself living there, away from the constant hassles of school and his lack of money. But beside the stove was the stack of tins Alex had been encouraged to 'borrow' when Chuck's cash had run out—they might as well have had 'shame' stamped on every one.

Alex took the few steps from the kitchen to the sleeping quarters but he was reluctant to move aside the overlapping sheets of tarpaulin. Chuck's top-of-the-range, feather stuffed sleeping bag would still be laid out on the pile of springy heather and bracken. Alex remembered the wide smile he'd been welcomed with when he'd last woken Chuck in the middle of the afternoon. But the nightmare of the faceless corpse caught in the seaweed made a dry retch stick in his throat.

Had Chuck been telling the truth about the blokes he'd said were searching for him? Had they found him? Alex felt panic surge through him again. All he needed to do was make sure there was nothing more of his or Daniel's lying around and get out quick.

His search over, he gave the site of the fateful fire a wider berth on his return to the boat. He was hurrying along now, keeping his head down. His eye was caught by a soft glint in the sand. He brushed the sand aside and picked up a pound coin. It could have been dropped by any of them, at any time, yet Alex knew it was the one Chuck had kept in his shorts' pocket. The one he took out whenever there was a decision to be made.

Alex tossed the coin and caught it in his hand. Well, there were no decisions to be made now. It was all over. He'd been stupid to get involved in the first place but he wasn't going to get dragged into the aftermath.

Moth was oblivious of the rising tide lapping at the boat when he got back. Alex let her sleep on as he pushed the boat out to sea and rowed back to the village.

CHAPTER 4

'No Alex today?'

Daniel, leaning against the fence, looked up at the girl speaking to him. 'Seems not.'

The girl, Caitlin, was in sixth year but Daniel had seen her in his physics class earlier in the day. She tipped her head.

'Sorry, that came out wrong,' he said. 'He was here first thing.' Daniel hadn't seen Alex since then and despite sending several texts during the day, Alex hadn't answered any of them. 'You missed your bus?' he asked, putting away his phone.

'No.' She laughed. 'I'm staying back to help out at youth club. Volunteering. For my CV.'

'Oh. I should do something like that, I suppose.'

'You won't have time in fifth year. It's crazy how much work you're expected to do in—what? —nine months.'

'I believe you!' Daniel said, feeling the weight on his shoulders of his overloaded backpack.

'You going to the shop?' Caitlin asked.

He shrugged. It was pointless hanging around at school. Whatever Alex was up to, he clearly wasn't going to put in an appearance now. Daniel nodded. 'Yeah. It's hot. I'll get a coke.'

He pushed himself off the fence and they ambled towards the village together, the younger kids racing past them.

In the shop, Daniel tagged along as Caitlin picked up Cheesy Wotsits, a Kit Kat Chunky and a Curly Wurly. He opened the fridge door for her and she took out an Irn Bru. Then, laughing, she put it back and stretched up for a carton of apple juice. Daniel could smell her spicy fragrance.

'One of my five a day, at least,' she said.

Daniel reached for a can of coke.

The line of customers waiting at the counter was made up of a mixture of tourists and locals and apart from a few polite pleasantries exchanged between them there was nothing of importance being gossiped about. Still, Daniel knew the big story of the day would be circulating around the village and what wasn't known for fact would be filled in along the way. He had to keep reminding himself that he'd done nothing wrong, and trust that whatever Alex was doing wouldn't cause them any further problems.

Daniel managed to avoid getting involved in conversation with anybody, keeping his head down, gaze averted, until they reached the counter. But as he was passing over money to pay for his drink, Halves came behind him to join the queue. His words were slurred but Daniel could tell what he was saying as he leaned in close. 'They reckon it was a teenager. Nobody we know.' Halves' breath was warm

26

in his ear. 'Saw your father driving up the road. That'll be him, then, heh? Rallying round.'

It was true. Any trouble in the parish always meant his father was called out to help. The new police constable had already dropped by at the Manse a few times. Daniel grunted in Halves' direction and followed Caitlin out of the shop.

'I've got ages till youth club starts. Do you fancy a paddle after this?' Caitlin asked as they stepped into bright sunshine.

Daniel took off his backpack and they sat together on the bench under the copper beech tree, each taking sips.

A paddle? Daniel considered what that would mean. If he rolled up the bottom of his jeans the blisters on his shins would still be covered.

'In the river?' he asked. He could cope with the river. The sea however ...

'Or the sea. Shame to waste this weather when we've been cooped up all day.'

Daniel knew how the rest of the conversation would go. He would say, the long beach? And she would say, how about that little cove? Isn't that where Alex keeps his boat? She wouldn't be the first girl to use him to get to Alex. Then Daniel would either have to say what a long walk it would be around the headland, or admit he couldn't get down the cliff path. Never mind his fear of the sea that he certainly didn't want to share with her. And all the while acting as if he didn't know that only this morning Chuck's dead body had washed up there.

Daniel shivered. And really, all Caitlin wanted was to see Alex.

'It doesn't matter,' Caitlin said.

And now he'd taken so long to say nothing she was getting bored with him.

Daniel drained his can and lobbed it at the recycle bin behind them. Tracing a clean arc, the can sailed through the circular opening.

'Cool,' Caitlin said. She scrunched her carton and got up to put it in the bin. She picked up her canvas bag with the goodies from the shop and swung it lazily to and fro.

Daniel re-shouldered his backpack, unsure if she was expecting him to say anything else. 'You want to come over to mine for a bit?' he asked.

Where had that come from? He never invited people home. People would go round from time to time—Alex, for instance. But Daniel couldn't remember ever actually asking anybody round, and certainly never a girl.

Seemingly Caitlin didn't think it at all unusual; she followed along as he took to the lane leading to the Manse, keeping his pace slow.

The Manse was a detached house in a crescent of other modern builds. They'd moved into the new house way back when the Old Manse became too dilapidated for the church Elders to maintain it any longer.

Daniel had loved their old house, butting as it did on to the church, sharing part of its garden with the graveyard.

He and Alex had been kids there, doing what kids do, building dens and camping out in canvas tents. But he'd got used to the new house. It was nearer the village, and when he'd started secondary school and such things mattered, he felt less like an oddity walking back to the modern house with its neatly trimmed hedges and geometrically planted shrubs.

They circled around the house to the back door. As they stepped into the empty kitchen where in the centre of a large wooden table scones were cooling on a wire tray, Daniel shook off his school shoes and pushed his feet into a pair of battered Converse.

'You want to come upstairs?' he asked.

Caitlin raised her eyebrows and gave a sly grin.

Daniel blushed. 'The living room is upstairs. Dad has his study in the front room. Where he takes people when they want a chat.'

'Oh. Okay.'

Daniel ushered Caitlin up the wide staircase. 'To the left,' he directed.

Caitlin turned at the top of the stairs and stood back to let Daniel push the door that was already open a little way. Eighties pop music was coming from a radio.

'So. How was first day back?' The voice came from a large woman standing by the window. She was ironing and didn't look up until Daniel and Caitlin had come right in. 'Not all bad then,' she said, eyeing Caitlin.

'Caitlin, this is Eva,' Daniel said quickly, to stem any further comments.

Eva stood the iron on end, crossed the room and reached out a mottled red hand.

'Pleased to meet you, Caitlin. It isn't often—'

'Lovely view you have here.'

Daniel gave a silent thanks for Caitlin's interruption.

Eva laughed. 'Makes doing the ironing easier, anyhow.' But then she turned to Daniel with a serious expression. 'Your father had to go out this afternoon.'

'Right,' Daniel answered. This was it. His father's absence would be to do with Chuck's body. This was where it all kicked off.

'He hopes to be back before supper,' Eva continued, glancing out of the window.

'Right.'

Eva regained her usual smile and shooed them both out of the living room. 'You go up to your room. I'll fetch you a cool drink. Squash all right for you, Caitlin?'

Daniel tried to tell her they'd had a drink at the shop but Caitlin spoke over him.

'That's really kind. We've some physics notes to decipher.'

'Clever girl too.' Eva winked at Daniel.

They climbed a narrow wooden staircase into an attic room. Daniel dropped his backpack beside his desk. Caitlin let her bag and jacket slide to the floor and stretched up to look out of the slanting window.

'Big house,' she said.

'We need a spare room. In case any of the church elders visit.'

Caitlin looked quizzical.

'You know, they have to stay over when they come out here.'

Caitlin gave a little laugh. Had he said something funny? Or was she laughing at him?

'Cool to have such important visitors,' she said.

'Dad lets other people stay in it ... sometimes.' Did he sound too defensive? It wasn't his fault his father was the church minister, or that they lived in a big house.

He pushed dirty socks into the basket that Eva emptied every other day and straightened the cover on his bed, wishing he could extend it over his chest of drawers too. So much clutter.

'Have a seat,' he said when he'd hidden the worst of his personal debris. He pulled out the desk chair.

Caitlin sat down and slipped off her sandals. 'Actually. Do you mind if we do go over those physics notes? It's a crash course for me ... I've not done physics since second year.'

Daniel didn't think he'd manage any of the physics homework. He'd not been able to concentrate on anything in classes all day. And he'd spent most of the lunchtime in different toilets and hidey-holes around school, texting Alex and avoiding speaking to anybody. All he'd been able to think about was the night of the fire, and how Chuck had stormed off when the plank gave way. It was the last time he'd seen Chuck alive.

Daniel pulled folders out of his bag and spread them on the desk. There was a gentle tapping at the door. Daniel opened it wide enough to accept the tray that Eva had brought up laid with glasses of squash and a plate with two buttered scones.

'Oh. Thanks,' Daniel said before quickly closing the door. He placed a glass on a wooden coaster in front of Caitlin and put the tray on the deep windowsill.

'Eva's not your mum, then?' Caitlin said after taking a long drink. She wasn't looking at him. She'd put down the glass and was flicking at the corner of the physics textbook.

Daniel felt himself flush. Eventually the words came. 'Mum died. Dad needs a housekeeper.' There wasn't much else to add.

Caitlin looked up at him. Her eyes narrowed slightly. 'I'm sorry ... about your mum.'

Daniel fumbled with the knot of his tie. 'Yeah.' He spoke in a rush, wanting to get things clear. 'She wasn't my real mum. Well, she was. I've never had another mum. But she wasn't—'

'You're adopted.' It wasn't a question. A simple statement of fact.

Daniel nodded, thankful that Caitlin didn't seem the sort to pry.

Caitlin opened the textbook and pressed her hand along the spine to stop the pages from closing again. Her long fingers had surprisingly knobbly knuckles. 'I hate all this stuff about electricity. Do you think there'll be much of it?' She pointed at the diagrams in the textbook.

While her eyes were firmly fixed on the book, Daniel gazed sideways at the slope of her chin, her pale skin at the neckline of her blouse. He shrugged. 'Seems to be a few chapters on it.'

As they worked together through the questions set, Caitlin took charge of the calculator and rapidly punched in numbers, scribbling the answers she got on a scrap of paper and showing them to Daniel before committing them to her jotter.

'Thanks for that,' she said before folding up her papers and stuffing them in her bag. 'I should have caught up over the summer. But ... I don't know ... the weeks drift by, don't they?'

Daniel closed his eyes. How he wished his summer holiday had drifted by.

He picked up Caitlin's jacket. 'Do you want to stay for supper? There's always plenty.'

Caitlin gave her little laugh again. Daniel decided he liked it. In fact, there were many things he decided he liked about her. And she hadn't mentioned Alex once since she'd been there.

'Another time. I said I'd help set up. Got to look keen.' She skipped down the stairs, her sandals slapping on the wood, and turned back to him. 'Thanks anyway. I'll see myself out.'

Then she disappeared, leaving Daniel wondering how he'd managed to tell so much about himself to somebody he'd barely spoken to before.

Daniel was closing the laptop on his desk when his father came in.

'Supper's almost ready. How was your day?'

'Fine.'

'I'm glad it was fine. And how about Alex?'

Daniel scrunched up the sheet of paper he and Caitlin had used to work out their calculations and aimed it at the waste bin. 'We're both great.' He pushed past his desk. 'If you don't mind ... I'm hungry. I'll go help Eva.'

Reverend Archie Macaulay picked up the abandoned tray from the windowsill. He straightened the Han Solo blind and sighed. On his way out, he stopped at the chest of drawers to prop up the framed photograph of his late wife that Daniel had knocked over in his rush to get out.

CHAPTER 5

Alex heard the whirr of the sewing machine as he stepped through the front door of the croft house. From the small square lobby, he stuck his head into his mum's workroom.

'Want a drink?' he called to her. Mum stopped sewing and a quiet descended. She was nodding her head, but not at Alex's question.

'Tony phoned. He said you left your jacket.'

Shit. Alex considered lying but made do with holding back on the truth.

'I dropped off a lobster.'

'Oh, I know that. He was very grateful. Said what a great lad you are.' She held him with her searching stare. 'Just how much time did you spend at school today?'

A difficult one.

'I had a job to do. Then ...'

'You promised, Alex. You promised to at least give it a go.'

He had promised. And he had fully intended to get to school. If he'd only emptied his creels and taken the catch to the hotel he might even have got there before the end of classes. But going out to Chuck's campsite had made him too late for that.

'I'll go tomorrow. They would only have been giving out books and things today.'

'Save your breath.' Mum turned back to her sewing, the motor growling as she pulled the stiff fabric this way and that.

'I'll make a start on tea.'

Taking the fiver from his trouser pocket, Alex lifted down the housekeeping tin from the top of the fridge and dropped it in, feeling bad that he'd allowed himself a five-pound phone top-up. He'd never get to save for decent fishing equipment—his dad's gear had long since been sold—while he was supplementing what his mum earned on the craft markets. It had been well over a year since his dad died but neither Alex nor his mum ever mentioned him. Dad had been unlucky; accidents happen. He shouldn't have been hand diving for scallops after that bout of flu. When the other divers had found him, he was already dead. Alex had a vision of his body drifting spread-eagled over the silty seabed.

Alex switched on his phone and propped it on the windowsill, the only place there was any chance of a signal at the croft. Immediately there was a stream of texts from Daniel. He only needed to open one to know the rest would be the same: 'Where are you?'

Aware that it would probably wind up Daniel even more, but not able to say much in a message, he texted back: 'At home'. He'd go around to the Manse as usual after tea.

Alex took tatties from a sack in the pantry, choosing the middle-sized ones that were easier to peel. Tuesday night—sausage and mash. And, if mum had remembered to go to the shop, red onion gravy.

* * *

After tea, Alex knocked on the back door of the Manse and, as usual, went straight in without waiting for an answer. Daniel was sitting reading at the kitchen table and Eva was stacking the dishwasher. Reverend Macaulay's voice was a low rumble from his study.

'Alex! Hello.' Eva welcomed him in. 'How's your mother? She'll be glad you're back at school.'

'Huh. Yeah. These are for you.' Alex handed over a box of eggs.

'Wonderful. I've some strawberries for you. Don't leave without them.'

Alex grunted a thanks.

'I brought this,' Daniel said, picking up a paperback from a pile of books on the dresser. 'We're starting with *Jean Brodie*.' Daniel copied their teacher's Edinburgh accent as he passed the book over. He sounded jokey enough but Alex could sense his temper fuming beneath the forced smile.

'Thanks. You read much of it yet?'

'We've to get to chapter three for tomorrow.'

'Right.' Alex dropped the book in the carrier bag he'd brought the eggs in. 'You coming out?'

Daniel left the kitchen and Alex could hear him in conversation with his father.

'Ready?' Daniel said when he came back in.

'What would you like in your sandwiches tomorrow?' Eva asked as Daniel held open the back door for Alex.

'Anything will do. Oh, if you've got any of that fruit bread left ...'

'Still waited on hand and foot, heh?' Alex said, aiming for a casual tone as they passed the woodlands behind the Manse.

Daniel shrugged, obviously saving himself until they were out of earshot.

'So where the fuck have you been all day?' he spat out when they'd reached their usual tree stump a little way up the hill.

There'd been a bench way back, but as bits had dropped off kids had used the wood to keep their poor attempts at fires going. The oak stump was wide enough for the two of them to sit side by side. Initials had been carved into all available surfaces along with comments on the distinguishing features of some of the locals.

'There's no need for—'

'What? It was you that insisted we had to get to school.' Daniel spat out the words. '"Give me till the end of the day," you said. Then you disappear, leaving me wondering what the hell's going on.'

'I know ... Sorry. But it was like I said.'

'Like what? And why am I having to ask you now?'

'I went back to the clifftop. All right? Mrs MacKinnon was on the beach. She ... she found him.'

'Yeah. I heard something about that,' Daniel responded in a more measured tone.

'What? At school?'

'Don't panic. I kept well away from the gossip.' Daniel stretched out his leg. 'But *that* didn't take you all day.'

Alex really didn't want to argue. And Daniel deserved some explanation. 'I went to the campsite. I wanted to make sure there was nothing of ours lying around.'

'That was your big plan? And I would have been a liability?'

'No. Well yes, I suppose you would have, like that.' Alex pointed at Daniel's leg. 'But I think you should stay out of it.'

'Fine by me.'

'And for your information, everything was just as we left it.'

They sat in silence for a while until Daniel said, 'I can't believe he's dead.'

'No.' Alex took a deep breath.

'It could have been one of us.'

'He must have had an accident. Chuck pushed things too far.'

Daniel gave him a sideways look. 'And we knew when to stop, did we?'

'Leave it, will you. We were stupid too. But there's no need for us to get involved from now on.'

'We pretend nothing happened,' Daniel said, making a point of putting his leg in a better position to ease the pain.

'How is the leg now, anyway?' Alex asked.

Daniel hitched up his jeans and prodded at the edge of a dressing on his shin. 'Shit sore.'

Alex recognised a thawing in Daniel's voice. The beginnings of a truce? 'Nothing's been said at home?' he said in a quieter voice.

'Eva has given me a few funny looks.' Daniel twisted his leg to get a view of the blister at the back of his knee that wasn't covered by a dressing.

'It doesn't look infected or anything,' Alex said.

'And you would know, how?'

'Well, you can hardly waltz into the doctor's with it, can you?'

Daniel didn't reply.

'We agreed.' Alex stood up and kicked the side of the tree stump. 'We tell nobody.'

Daniel straightened his jeans and stood next to Alex; together they took in the view over the loch.

'But what about when the police come round? What will we tell them?'

'We tell them nothing ... and they might not come.'

'You what? They've got a dead body on their hands. Even with an accident they'll make enquiries. A boy a bit older than us.' Daniel paused before adding. 'They'll come all right.'

Alex found a stick and started to beat the fronds of bracken growing nearby. 'They'll work out who he is without us telling them. They don't need us. We can keep quiet.' They could get through this if they stuck together.

'And if they ask what we were doing over the summer...?'

'We'll get our stories straight. Like I said. No way can my mum find out.'

The wind dropped and midges began to ditz around them. Daniel pulled up his hood. 'What did he look like?'

'What? You mean ... his body?'

Daniel nodded.

Alex stuffed his hands in his jacket pockets. 'Horrible. His legs all stuck out. And ... all the flesh on his face was gone ... like something had been eating at him or he'd smashed against the rocks ... and the stink.'

'No face?'

Alex shook his head.

'But it was Chuck?'

'Oh, it was Chuck all right,' Alex said.

WEDNESDAY

CHAPTER 6

Sport and Recreation had been shit. Hospitality even more shit. As for English—last night Alex's eyes had closed before he'd read more than a few pages of the novel Daniel had brought back for him. Going to school was bad enough—he didn't want to read about a bunch of weird girls going to school in Edinburgh. Girls who thought rebellion was altering how they wore their hats, for God's sake. Girls who could be herded by a few boys on bikes. Mr Frome hadn't expected Alex to answer any of the questions he'd volleyed at the class that morning and although Alex wanted to prove himself up to higher English, today that suited him just fine.

There was plenty of chat going on in the corridors at lunchtime about the 'dead kid on the beach' as everyone was calling Chuck's body. Alex and Daniel kept away from the gossip and headed out to the football pitch—not that there was anything unusual in that—where the noise of the girls and boys yelling at each other for the ball gave them space.

Alex had finished most of his sandwich before they'd even left the building but Daniel waited until they'd sat at the side of the pitch before he took the lid off his lunchbox to use as a makeshift plate. Staring straight ahead, Alex watched from the corner of his eye as Daniel did his usual act of nibbling the crusts off the triangular sandwiches before working his way round and round until there was only a tiny piece left. While eating, putting the sandwich down between bites, Daniel pulled out a geography textbook from his backpack and was intermittently writing notes in the margins.

Daniel had hardly spoken to him all morning other than to moan about the amount of work being doled out and Alex hadn't felt inclined to humour him. But when Daniel lifted the middle section of his lunchbox to reveal two pieces of buttered fruit loaf and silently handed a piece to Alex, Alex polished it off in two mouthfuls.

At the end of school Alex left the woodwork portacabin and saw Daniel in the bus queue.

'I'm going back to Caitlin's,' Daniel said, blushing slightly as he sidled over to Alex. 'We're doing chemistry.' Alex raised his eyebrows. 'Her dad has got Book Club tonight. He'll drive me back. You coming to mine after tea?'

'Book Club.' Alex's response was flat.

'Yeah. Actually, I thought we might join. What do you think?'

Alex didn't answer, but the bus engine revved and Daniel limped hurriedly back to the diminishing queue where Caitlin was waiting for him.

CHAPTER 7

'Book Club?'

'You don't need to keep on.' Daniel hadn't expected Alex to welcome the suggestion, but Caitlin was showing an interest in him and he was going to take full advantage of it. Sitting on the edge of his bed, giving his attention to lifting the tape holding the dressings on his leg, he squeezed the tube of Germolene and rubbed the pink cream around the edges of his blisters. 'I thought you wanted to get better at English. It's only once a month.' He gave a quick glance at Alex who was swinging around in the desk chair. It creaked in a slow rhythm.

When Alex spoke again his tone wasn't any friendlier. 'So. Caitlin Macgregor.'

'So? So what?'

'She's in S6.'

'She's also in my physics class. And she did higher chemistry last year. She's helping me with the calculations.'

'Very cosy.' Alex rocked in the chair now, backwards and forwards, the squeaks getting louder and faster, driving his words. 'And her dad goes to Book Club. In fact, he's there right now. I'm surprised you didn't go in with him if you want to join so much.'

'Just what's your problem?' Daniel rolled up his shirtsleeve to examine the bruises on his arm that were morphing from their original purple to a yellowy green. A few more days wearing long sleeve shirts then.

'Me? No problems. None whatsoever.' Alex planted his feet firmly on the carpeted floor, bringing his rocking to an abrupt halt.

Daniel returned the Germolene to the top drawer of his bedside cabinet and pushed Alex out of the desk chair. He sat at the desk himself and opened his laptop.

Obviously in no rush to leave, Alex jumped on to Daniel's bed and stretched out, cupping his hands behind his head. 'And what about tomorrow?'

Daniel ignored the question.

'Will you be helping each other out tomorrow after school?'

'Fucksake, Alex. You know very well I won't. Tomorrow's Thursday.'

'Just checking.'

'I'll be there. As usual.'

Then Alex noticed the empty space on the wall by Daniel's bed. 'Hey. Where's our main man gone?'

Daniel continued clicking keys on his laptop.

'Don't tell me ... the cute lassie doesn't think much of AC/DC.'

'We haven't discussed music preferences.'

'Just your gut feeling she's more a Chase & Status girl.'

'Look, I need to get on with this chemistry now.'

'Aye, before you forget all the answers Miss "Oh me? I'm going to be a psychologist" has told you.' Alex jumped to his feet. 'And I've got to get the hens in. A pine marten was hanging around last night.'

* * *

From his sloping window Daniel watched Alex climb over the fence and head up the hill towards the croft. Back at his desk and safe in his seclusion Daniel opened his email account, tapping in his password. A dark bold entry showed there was a new message from Ellie. Emailing was the only way Daniel had ever communicated with her. He preferred it that way. The other occasional emails he received were mostly from the librarian, so it felt like his and Ellie's own private forum. Over the last month since she'd first contacted him she'd shared a lot of her life story. She'd had a rough time moving from one set of foster carers to another. Daniel was luckier. He'd been a baby when the reverend and his wife adopted him.

He'd spent hours re-reading her messages several times over to try and understand what she'd had to cope with— was coping with still. He didn't open the new mail immediately but scrolled up the screen to the message she'd sent yesterday.

Hi Danny,

*You sound so clever—all those science
subjects you're taking! Not like me. I wasn't
too bad at art but you could say school
and me didn't agree. LOL I'm a poet and
didn't know it. My foster parents tried to
get me to study. You know, bribed me, or
grounded me when I didn't come home at
night. They try harder at things like that,
don't you think? Making out they're really
strict. Or maybe it's just mine. Yours sound
a bit more normal. Oh though, sorry. I
forgot about your mum. Bet she was lovely.
Not like the old biddy I'm with. I'll have
to sign off now, got to sign on tomoz. LOL.
Need to be up early.*

Ellie

His replies to her messages were only ever a couple of
lines but that didn't stop her rambling on to him. He felt
ready to open her new message.

Hi Danny,

*Guess what. I'm going to Perth tomorrow.
Clothes shopping. Don't get too excited.
It's only with Mum. And not for proper
clothes—not things I can wear going out.
She's got me an interview. It's only in a
cafe. Probably washing up. Have to look*

willing though to keep getting my Magners vouchers.

I looked up that shinty on the internet. It looks mental. Some fit fellas though. I've got brown eyes. What about you?

Ellie

Ellie had suggested exchanging photographs earlier on, but Daniel hadn't answered that message and she hadn't mentioned it again. He hit 'Reply' and started his message:

Hi Ellie,

Yes, brown eyes. Dark brown hair.

He deleted the *'Dark brown hair'* and continued:

I'm a bit of a fraud at shinty. I scored a lucky goal one day from half way up the pitch. That bought me some kudos.

He deleted *'kudos'* and replaced it with *'respect'*.

We've got a match on Saturday but I'm not sure I'll be able to play. I hurt my leg a few days ago, which makes running a bit difficult. Hope your interview goes well. That is if you want the job.

Daniel

He read through his reply. He wanted to tell her about meeting Caitlin. About how good it was to have someone to go over homework with—and how he secretly thought

Caitlin might like him. But there was no way he could have told her about Chuck's body turning up on the beach and all the problems that promised. Even though he hadn't seen the body, he couldn't bring himself to talk about it—not even to his twin sister.

THURSDAY

CHAPTER 8

Alex picked up his copy of *The Prime of Miss Jean Brodie* from his bedside table. He'd still only read half of the set chapters. Two days in to the new term and he was already getting behind the rest of the class. Maybe Daniel's idea about reading more wasn't such a stupid idea after all. But then again, what use would a pointless English higher be anyway?

What was the use of anything anymore? He wanted to tear the pages out of the stupid book and throw it across the room, but instead he tossed it from hand to hand before stuffing it to the bottom of his rucksack.

He took a few paces up and down his bedroom to calm down. He needed to keep his cool, but the vision of Chuck's body at the foot of the cliffs was on repeat play. Alex didn't need to know how Chuck had died. Really, he didn't. But try telling his brain that.

Rootling through the pile of clothes on the floor, he sorted out his shinty gear. That got crammed into his bag too, ready for the training session after school.

Mum stuck her head around his bedroom door. 'Don't forget I'll be home late.' She screwed up her nose as Alex retrieved a pair of boxers from under the duvet and lobbed them onto the pile of washing he was kicking together at the end of his bed. 'Wish me luck getting rid of this lot,' she added, holding out an armful of colourful rag dolls.

'You want me to help load the van?' Alex asked, stepping into the square landing between the two bedrooms.

'There's a boxful in the workroom. You could bring that out.'

The boot of the van was open and Alex tottered barefoot across the tarmac path carrying the cardboard box.

'Shall I make soup tonight?' Alex asked with his head in the back of the small van. It had previously been used to cart Dad's diving gear but now took homemade toys to craft fairs throughout the summer months.

His mum waved one of the rag doll arms at him. 'How would I ever manage without you? That'd be great.'

Alex watched the van rattle across the cattle grid and poke out into the single-track road that ran in front of their croft. Going back to his bedroom, he finished getting ready for another pointless day at school.

Shinty training started at five. Daniel arrived early. It was cooler in the changing room and Daniel filled a washbasin with cold water before dunking his face in it in an attempt to shift the ache across his forehead.

Despite the changing room being empty, he went into a cubicle to change. He lifted a corner of the dressing covering the largest blister; the skin around it had turned a dark red. Twisting his leg, he saw pus seeping through livid cracks at the back of his knee. No way could he wear shorts. But even though the heat of the day had hardly lessened, he wouldn't be the only one wearing trackies; some of the other lads regularly got teased about their skinny legs.

As Daniel rambled onto the pitch he watched Alex take feeds from other kids who'd been hanging around since the end of the school day. Alex was a natural keeper, his caman shot out with lightning speed to stop incoming balls.

'Over here,' Alex called to him.

Daniel joined him and they turned away, walking together alongside the fence.

'You going to manage with your leg?' Alex asked.

'Suppose.'

'I'll see if I can get us off soonish.'

'Whatever.'

Alex peered around, checking they couldn't be overheard. 'We need to talk.'

'We do?' Daniel said, picking up a stray shinty ball and bouncing it on his caman.

'Get our stories straight. You know. In case the police—'

'If you say so.'

Alex pulled Daniel closer. 'What is it with you? I thought you'd want to sort this out.'

'I should never have gotten involved,' Daniel said as he walked away with a stiff-legged stride.

Within a few minutes the pitch was filled with lads and girls warming up, stretching their calf muscles and running around the perimeter fence. Daniel was mostly left to himself and managed to jog on the spot when any attention came his way. Back in second year, when they'd both joined the shinty training sessions, Alex had told him he just needed to keep scoring the goals to keep a place in the team. That was easy for Alex to say. But a place in the team was one way to deflect the bullying that had hounded him for as long as he could remember. Over the seasons his skills and his stamina had improved as he ran continuously up and down the wing giving him an advantage over the heavier, tougher guys.

'Ready positions,' Coach bellowed after blowing his whistle to gather the players around him. 'Daniel, Eilish, hands further apart. Rory! Top hand, knuckles up!'

Daniel joined in with the regular drills that Coach put them through before they started a game. But with each step, with each stretch, the pain in his right leg was getting worse. Soon it would be unbearable. He could feel the blister tightening and pulling. Sweat gathered on his forehead and ran into his eyes. He wiped his face with the back of his hand.

'And into dribbling.' Coach's voice boomed around Daniel's skull. Daniel pushed out his caman to control the ball ahead of him but his hands were trembling. He stumbled over his feet and crashed to the ground.

'I never even touched him,' said a girl's voice to his left.

A hand grasped his elbow. Alex was at his side helping him to his feet.

'I'm not feeling very good,' Daniel said in a whisper.

'All right, Daniel?' Coach came running over and peered into Daniel's face. 'Get him a drink of water, Alex. This heat is ridiculous.'

Alex sprinted off the pitch and Daniel stumbled after him. In the changing room Daniel sat on the wooden bench, leaning the back of his head against the cold breezeblock wall, while Alex filled his water bottle.

'You get back now,' Daniel said, taking sips from the water bottle. 'I'll be fine.'

But Alex had pulled out a pile of paper towels from the dispenser and was holding them under the cold tap. 'You're burning up,' he said crossing the room and pressing the wet towels to Daniel's forehead.

The rivulets of cool liquid ran down his face and onto his chest. He shivered as the water soaked his t-shirt. 'I tell you, I'm all right,' he said pushing Alex's arm away.

'You can't go back home yet ... Eva will suspect something. You can come to mine. Mum won't be back until well after training has finished.' Alex was talking fast. 'Do you need any painkillers? Mum'll have some.'

Daniel slumped down on the bench. 'You wanted to talk,' he managed to say in a low voice.

'Not now. Not while you're like this,' Alex said, hovering around him.

'Tell me. How did it happen? What went wrong?'

'What?'

'How did he die?'

'You don't need to think about that,' Alex said, sitting beside him.

'How can you *not* think about it? I can't stop!' Daniel screwed up his eyes. 'What do you reckon happened?'

'I don't know. Really. I've no idea.'

'Did he fall off the cliff? Hit his head? Did he drown?' Daniel tried to get up but his head was spinning.

'You know as much as I do. I didn't see him after Saturday night.'

'When I fell.'

Alex looked away. 'I tried my best. Got you home.'

'Pity you asked me to go in the first place.' Daniel staggered to his feet but Alex grabbed his arm and made him sit down again.

After a few moments Alex said, 'You needn't have joined in.'

'I had no choice. Did I?'

Alex didn't answer.

'I said—'

'I know what you said ... You had a choice.'

'"You want to be that kid that never takes a dare?" That's what you said.' He got to his feet and this time Alex didn't stop him.

'You'll be better in a couple of days.' Alex reached out and grabbed Daniel's wrist.

Daniel shook off Alex's hand just as a lad with spiky hair sauntered in. 'Okay, lover boys. Coach wants to know how wimpy kid is.'

'We're just coming,' Daniel said before Alex could answer.

The lad blew a kiss at them, turned and left them alone.

CHAPTER 9

That Shane was one creepy guy but Caitlin knew Fetch Walker could handle him no problem. Caitlin let Fetch drain neon gas energy from another advertising sign before leaping to the next tower block at crazy speed. Wow, that was some move. Caitlin's game plan was for Fetch to gain as many skill points as possible. Regular boosts of energy and a maximum skill level was the best way to get the most out of the game.

Caitlin had sneaked this *inFAMOUS: First Light* standalone game in with a book order that'd been delivered a few days ago. She'd set out with good intentions of only playing after homework was completed for the day, but she'd hit a tricky physics question and had found herself easily distracted. For some reason, her concentration wasn't exactly at its best in this alternative world either—she'd missed several easy targets.

Gazing out of her bedroom window she watched her father heading out to the compost bin. She quit the game and went back to her physics textbook. But no matter how long she stared at the physics question, the numbers made no sense at all. How would knowing how to calculate the voltage across the thermistor be of any use to her as a psychologist? She knew well enough that the extra science with a predicted grade A would make all the difference on her UCAS application. But physics? Really? She knew the answer to that argument too. It was rammed home that content didn't matter; it was the ability to study hard, get the grades, beat the competition with her personal statement.

Still. Surely she was allowed some free time. Time to pursue other interests. She scrolled through the pictures on her phone until she reached the one she'd taken, surreptitiously, of Daniel sitting under the beech tree two days ago after school.

She pushed back her chair, ruckling her bedside rug, and headed downstairs. The rest of the family were busy in the kitchen and nobody paid her attention until she reached up to take the lead from the back of the kitchen door. With the slight clink of the metal chain, Banjo, his huge body overflowing from his basket by the sink, raised his head.

'Thought I'd take Banjo for a walk,' Caitlin said to nobody in particular.

Her mother turned to face her but kept her forefinger on the page she was scanning; she pushed up her glasses to peer questioningly at Caitlin.

'No need,' Dad said, 'I took him for a long walk this morning. He was whacked after that. It's this heat.'

But Banjo was already on his feet having heard the word 'walk', as Caitlin had predicted. His long tail caused so much of a draught as he batted it to and fro that her mother slapped her hand on her papers to stop them flying off the table.

'I'll come too,' Caitlin's younger sister Corrine said, pushing her own jotter across the kitchen table.

'Well, if you've finished your maths...' Dad said, halting a moment from chopping carrots.

No way. As close as Caitlin was to her sister, who was already beginning to see the attractions of the opposite sex, this was not a walk where she wanted company.

Inwardly apologising to Corrine for what she was about to do, Caitlin stumbled past the now woofing Banjo, leaned across the table and picked up the jotter. After a quick scan she said, 'You might want to look at number six.'

It worked like a charm. Dad scurried over and snatched up the jotter.

'Oh for goodness sake, Corrine. You know how to divide fractions by now.'

Caitlin clipped on Banjo's lead and was out the back door before anybody could say another word.

It was a couple of miles over the high road to the shinty pitch. She could be there before training finished, even with Banjo sticking his nose into every hole he could find.

Once she'd gained some height through the community woodlands and had left the public path Caitlin reined in Banjo's extending lead and unclipped it from his collar. Free from his leash, Banjo charged a few mad dashes away then rushed back, jumping wildly around her. 'Do you really have to be quite so frantic,' she said, ruffling the fur on his back.

Together they skirted a burn with its trickle of water making a way through stones and tree roots. Banjo slithered down the bank and, with his front paws submerged, began slurping up the water.

Caitlin took a few strides up onto the common grazings and swore. Dotted along the skyline was a scattering of highland cattle. Even with his lead on Caitlin didn't fancy taking Banjo through that lot.

Take Banjo home and come back on her own? Drop down on to the main road? That would add on another mile at least.

'Shit,' she said again walking back to the burn where Banjo was now lifting stones with his teeth and letting them fall into the water, causing mini tidal waves on the sandy bank. Caitlin sat beside Banjo, took off her trainers and socks and dipped her toes into the stinging cold water. Sensing another game, Banjo leaped towards her and tugged at the socks in her hand. She tugged back, feeling the vibrations of Banjo's bass growls that rose from his excitement.

'Boys,' she said, eventually tiring of Banjo's game. 'Are they ever worth the effort.'

It was as she was clipping the lead back on to his collar that Banjo started to bark. His previous playful rumble switched to a serious growl from the back of his throat. His muzzle quivered. Before Caitlin had chance to look around for what had spooked him, a boy wearing sports gear crashed towards them through the undergrowth.

'Lost,' the boy said through quick shallow breaths, coming to a stop beside her. 'Which way to the road?'

Caitlin didn't recognise him. With his athletic build he might be from a cross-country running team or some such. But there was something unsettling about him. His dark set eyes and blonde hair reminded her of an albino badger she'd once seen. And what was with that ostentatious earring? She pulled Banjo closer to her. 'You can join the path in about twenty metres,' she said pointing towards the community woods but keeping her eyes fixed on the boy. 'Then take a right at the bottom.'

He gave her a beaming smile and a thumbs up before sprinting off in the direction she'd given.

She waited a few minutes before heading down the same path herself. She saw nobody else on the route home and as she took the track leading to their back garden she could hear Corrine practising her fiddle outside.

'Banished out here to torment the birds then, Corrie.' Caitlin tried a conciliatory tone as she opened the garden gate, but Corrine was having none of it.

'That was a mean trick,' Corrine said, pausing mid-scale.

'Yeah, well...'

'And you'd missed him anyway.' Corrine said, starting up a highland reel on her fiddle, playing at a furious tempo.

'Missed who?' Caitlin called above the din, but she stopped short as her dad came out of the back door holding a book.

'Seems *somebody* wants you to do well in physics,' Dad was saying as he thumbed through the pages, clearly holding back a knowing wink and making do with waggling his eyebrows on the "somebody". 'He must have left it earlier. It was in the front porch. Full of handmade notes too.'

Caitlin felt her face flush. Maybe inviting Daniel back to hers yesterday had been a mistake if Dad was going to act so excruciatingly unsubtle. 'Thanks,' she said taking the textbook off Dad and running upstairs to her room. Everything else would have to wait; what Caitlin needed right now to calm herself down before dinner was to take Fetch Walker through a couple of missions.

CHAPTER 10

Alex considered. How was he going to get Daniel home? They'd stopped again and Daniel had lowered himself awkwardly onto the grassy verge at the side of the road. He stretched his sore leg out uncomfortably in front of him, squashing the daisies. They'd walked barely a quarter of a mile in the last ten minutes and there was at least another mile to the village.

Alex had persuaded Daniel to take painkillers before they'd left the shinty pitch. Trying not to interrupt the training session that had barely got started, he'd picked out a girl in pristine kit practicing dribbling. She'd given him a couple of paracetamols from her bag.

But Daniel seemed even redder in the face now. Was it just the mood he was in or some sort of infection? Alex knew his mum had recently been prescribed some antibiotics that she'd never finished.

'I'll not take them,' Daniel answered, clamping his mouth firmly shut when Alex suggested getting them.

'All right. I'm hardly going to force feed them to you.'

'There're all different types, you know.' Daniel readjusted the position of his leg and accepted the water bottle Alex held out for him.

'Well, they wouldn't do you any harm would they? You need something. And if they did work...'

'Leave it, will you.'

Alex was running out of options. 'I'll take you to the doc's then.'

'For God's sake, I'm seventeen next week not seven. I don't need you to *take* me anywhere.'

'Yeah. You're right. Be better if I'm not hanging around. You can make up something. And your dad and Eva won't know anything.'

'Or I could tell the truth.'

Alex laughed as Daniel hoisted himself up. An uncertain laugh. 'But you won't ... heh?'

They set off again along the single-track road and, as they got into a regular paced rhythm, Alex thought Daniel was wincing with pain less and managing to put his foot down for longer.

They stopped again at the ford where Alex would normally cross the river and take the track to his croft and Daniel would walk on along the river to the village. Even though Daniel was definitely walking better now Alex wondered if he should make an excuse for going to the village himself—to the shop maybe?

'I'll be all right. You go home,' Daniel said, obviously aware of Alex's concern. He took his weight on his good leg and lifted the other, waggling his foot as if to shake the pain out.

'How about I see you down to the main road? Nothing comes up here ... if you fall or...'

Daniel hopped off the track and sat on a large boulder. 'Will you listen to me—just for once. I'm walking to the village—alone. I'm going to the surgery to get my leg seen to and then I'm going home. I don't need a minder for that.' He put an elbow on his good knee and rested his head in his hand.

Alex stood watching the sun skirt the tops of the hills on the other side of the river. He could make out the white gable end of his house. He'd be back home in less than ten minutes. It would take Daniel ages to get to the village. Alex couldn't stand the thought of rattling around the croft, getting the tea ready, and all the while worrying about Daniel.

'All right, on you go,' Alex said eventually. 'I'll give you a call later.' He stretched a hand out to help Daniel get up.

'No!' Daniel stood up suddenly. 'Leave it.'

Alex raised his hands in the air, like a gangster caught by the cops. 'Whoa. Keep your hair on.'

Daniel pushed out his chin. 'You don't get it, do you? I've had enough, Alex.'

'You'll be better in a couple of days ... with some antibiotics.'

'I know I will. But what if I have to miss school because of all this?' Daniel's forehead creased. 'We're not kids anymore. We can't keep playing games. Dangerous games.'

'But you agreed ... You agreed that we needed to challenge our minds, challenge our bodies. To know what we're made of.'

'You really believed all that garbage Chuck gave us, didn't you?' Daniel waved his arms around wildly. '"*The passage into manhood.*"'

Alex nodded slowly, stunned. 'So what are you saying?'

'Like I said. I've had enough. It was Chuck who was the danger all along—but you wouldn't see that, would you? All you could see was his six-pack.'

Alex felt his neck redden. 'We both had doubts. We talked through them. We decided we wanted to do it.'

'Yeah. We both had doubts. That's why I stuck around to make sure you didn't do anything too stupid.'

'You stuck around...?'

Daniel nodded. 'Don't like that idea? The thought of having a minder? Yet you're happy to think you have to watch over me,' he said with a sneer. 'Now you know what it feels like.'

'Fuck you then,' Alex said, putting his foot on the first large stepping-stone across the river. 'I'll see you around.' Without looking back, he splashed across the ford.

Daniel rubbed his face and wiped the sweat from the back of his neck. A few minutes' rest before heading home was all he needed. He slithered down the riverbank and stared into the flowing water, mesmerised by the small fishes whirling in and out of the weeds at the edge of the river. So he didn't hear the group of lads coming down the road.

He did feel the thump in the small of his back though.

'You want to settle a bet?' Neil, the largest of the bunch, twisted Daniel's arm up his back. 'I say you're planning how to top yourself, but Action here reckons you're making up poetry.'

'Piss off,' Daniel said, not bothering to look around.

'Ha ha. Good one, Brainiac,' Neil said, letting go of Daniel's arm after giving it a final twist.

Daniel turned to face them.

But another of the bunch, Seamus, moved in and pushed him in the shoulder until he staggered back. 'Oooh. Got suddenly brave, have we? And no bum friend to help you out? Where's he gone? At home watching re-runs of Strictly?'

'Why should I care where he is?'

'Had a tiff, have you?' another lad taunted. 'Didn't you learn the steps right?'

Daniel heard a snap, then saw Seamus point an airgun at the ground not far from his feet. 'Here, I'll teach you a few.' He pulled the trigger. The report echoed from the surrounding hills as the pellet raised stones and dust from the path.

'You're crazy,' Daniel said, backing away.

The lads crowded in.

'You're cr ...crazy,' Seamus mocked.

Daniel hadn't stuttered. Not like that. For some reason this injustice made him angrier than the physical provocations. 'Piss off,' he yelled, ready, in his head at least, to square up to any of them.

'Not a very nice way to speak to mates,' Seamus said as he shoved Daniel further and further back.

And with no physical strength to retaliate, Daniel stumbled over the rough ground and landed on his back in the river.

The lads were laughing as they sauntered off, leaving Daniel to his watery humiliation.

Alex heard the rebounding echoes of the shot as he stepped into the cool of the lobby of the croft but paid little attention to it. The local rabbit population was enjoying the hot weather in its own way and there were plenty of folk who used the creatures either for target practice or for a pie filling. He scuffled his toe into the pile of post on the mat before bending down to sort out the couple of white envelopes from amongst the catalogues and junk mail.

That was all he needed. He'd forgotten the phone bill would be arriving this week. He quickly opened the envelope and looked immediately at the bold numbers at the bottom of the first page. It took him a moment to register the full amount. Lucky he'd got home first. What had Mum been doing? There was a load of calls to random numbers he was sure had never appeared on bills before.

Up in his bedroom Alex switched on his computer, logged in to his PayPal account and checked his balance. He opened a bookmarked favourite in another tab and scrolled down the page, reciting the spec of the new outboard motor he dreamed of buying: *Recoil start with 6 amp charging coil; 4-Stroke OHC—2 cylinders; 222cm3 displacement; 8 hp @ 5000 rpm.* Over a grand, even second-hand. There was no chance of getting it when he couldn't even afford to pay the household bills. He shrugged the tension out of his shoulders and closed the tab.

Stretching to the top of the bedroom doorframe, he let his fingertips find the desk drawer key then opened the drawer and took out the webcam. Even before Dad's accident they hadn't been rolling in cash but Mum had insisted that Alex needed a computer for his homework. It was the lowest spec model, even back then, but he could plug in a webcam.

Next he took a curly black wig out of the drawer. Chuck had looked at him in disbelief when Alex voiced his wonder at why Chuck should own a wig. Didn't Alex know anything about how protected witnesses were moved around the country? In a safe place now, Chuck wouldn't need it until he appeared in court next. Alex could borrow it, Chuck had said, passing it over to Alex with the list of websites.

Alex went through to Mum's bedroom to get what he needed there before going into the bathroom.

The sun superheated the small space and Alex fought with the metal catch to open the window. Pulling the hand towel off the rickety chair, he swatted at a lone bluebottle. It hit the windowsill and whizzed around on its back amidst the corpses of its smaller cousins.

Moving to the sink to look into the tiny mirror Alex felt his stomach tighten, heard it grumble in complaint about what he was going to do. Still, best not to think too much. He stripped off his t-shirt, threw it in the bath and set to work. It didn't usually take long and if he could keep his five-star rating he'd be able to increase his fee. He held out his hand until the trembling reduced then carefully applied the black eyeliner and mascara before pulling the wig over his close-cropped ginger stubble—until he was completely unrecognisable as Alex Cameron. He ferreted in the cupboard under the sink for Mum's lavender body oil, squelched a globule into one hand and rubbed his palms together before massaging the oil into his upper arms, making his biceps glisten.

He'd used tweezers the first time, on Chuck's recommendation, to remove the few hairs from his chest. He wasn't going to do that again in a hurry. And on the webcam the few hairs that had since corkscrewed out between his pectorals didn't show up anyway.

Twenty minutes later, after a thorough shower, he checked that his PayPal account was £20 up.

He was in the kitchen making soup when he heard a vehicle on the track. It was the right time for Mum to be getting back but he could tell from the rattle of the vehicle over the rough stones that it wasn't the Corsa van. A glance out of the window confirmed it. Going through the back door he stooped to pick up one of Mum's rag dolls that lay sprawled next to an empty plant pot. How had he missed that when he'd come home, with its bright gingham dress and garishly rosy cheeks?

The police van changed its tone to a low rumble as it reached the tarmac drive leading to the back door. The policewoman behind the wheel had only been in the area for a short while. As she stepped out of the van there was no hint of a smile. This wasn't a 'getting to know you' call.

CHAPTER 11

'Hello ... It's Alex, if I remember rightly?' the police officer said, smoothing down her trousers.

She'd visited the school before the summer holidays and Alex had been roped into showing her round. He was impressed if she'd remembered his name since then. He nodded as he stood beside the croft door to meet her.

'Constable Logan,' she announced as she approached. 'Is your mum about?'

Alex relaxed a little. Maybe it was Mum she wanted to see. He tucked the rag doll under his arm. 'She should be back soon. Do you want to come in and wait?'

Constable Logan looked directly at Alex. 'I wanted to chat to you actually.' She hesitated. 'But I can come back when your mum's here.'

'There's no need.' Alex returned her direct stare. 'What do you want?'

'Well ...'

Alex watched Constable Logan's face as she thought for a moment.

'If you're sure? It shouldn't take long.'

Alex shrugged.

'Shall we step inside?' She nodded towards the door.

As they entered the lobby Alex indicated the way into the kitchen where the soup pan lid was rattling.

Constable Logan glanced around. 'You'll have heard about the body found on the beach.'

Alex was glad she didn't make small talk first. With luck he'd be able to answer whatever questions she had before his mum came back. 'Yeah. I heard something about it in the shop.'

'Hmm.' Constable Logan placed her hands on the back of a kitchen chair and leaned forward. 'Formal identification might take some time due to the nature of the ...' For the first time she looked a bit uncomfortable. But she went on. 'The cove where we found ... That's where you moor your boat?'

Alex nodded.

'And you took your boat out on Tuesday?'

'Yeah ... Shit.' He grimaced, hoping she would take it as an apology for swearing in front of her. 'We must have been quite close when we crossed the beach.'

Constable Logan picked up on the word, as he hoped. 'We?'

'Me and my cousin, Moth—'

'Moth?'

'Her name is Eilish ... but she likes to party ... You know, late at night.' Alex gave a short laugh, but Constable Logan's face remained straight as she indicated for him to carry on with his story.

'She helped me with the creels. When we came back, I saw part of the cove was taped off.'

'So then ...?'

'I had to go to the harbour. I'd dropped off a lobster at the hotel but when I rowed back to my mooring in the cove we were stopped by a couple of your lot. I had to row back to the village and tie her up there ... I've been in school the last couple of days so she's still there.'

'That's fine—'

'Well, it's not really,' Alex interrupted. 'She's in the way. I'll be checking my creels again tomorrow and I'll get her back to the cove ... if that's all right with you.'

PC Logan turned to look out of the kitchen window before answering. 'That should be okay.'

Alex moved towards the door. The interview hadn't gone too badly.

But, clearly, Constable Logan hadn't finished and she stood her ground. 'What I wanted to ask you, Alex ... You know all the young folk around here. We've had no reports of anybody missing locally.' She hesitated for a moment. 'I was wondering if you'd seen any people hanging around in the area recently. Say in the last couple of weeks?'

Alex could feel sweat pool at the base of his spine. He gave what he hoped was a noncommittal shrug. 'There's always folk coming and going. To work in the caravan park ... or the fish farms,' he said.

'And you didn't see anybody else that morning? — Tuesday morning—around the clifftops?'

Alex pictured the heather and gorse bushes, the path cutting through. 'No. Nobody.'

'Well ... Okay, thanks.' This time Constable Logan followed Alex out of the kitchen. 'Tell your mum I called, won't you?'

As Constable Logan ducked into the driving seat of her van Alex leaned against the back door and took a deep breath. Formal identification could take some time, she'd said. And then, well, hopefully there'd be no need for them to look too closely at the jumper Chuck had been wearing.

Alex waited until the police van had clattered its way off the croft then headed in to message Daniel and let him know that Constable Logan was doing the rounds. But the sound of another vehicle on the road stopped him at the bottom of the stairs; this time it was the Corsa van.

CHAPTER 12

Daniel quickly went to the bathroom and filled a tumbler with water. Back in his bedroom, he pushed two of the antibiotic pills the doctor had given him out of their blister pack and swallowed them together. He sprawled across his bed and balanced his laptop on his rumpled duvet. But when he heard the shush, shush of his father's slippers mounting the wooden staircase to his room Daniel quickly closed his laptop and fished out the *Loaded* mag from under his pillow. He lay back and pulled the duvet up to his chin.

His father poked his head around the door following a tentative knocking.

Daniel dropped the magazine to the floor. 'A bit of privacy please,' Daniel said and wondered if his cheeks were blushing sufficiently.

'Oh. Right. I'm just checking you've remembered I'll be away until Monday. I'll be leaving early in the morning,' his father said from the doorway.

'I've remembered.'

'I can ask Eva to call in over the weekend.'

'No. There's no need. She'll leave enough food to feed the whole village anyway.'

His father took a step into the room. 'It's roasting in here. Shall I open the window,' he said but stopped as he glanced down at Daniel and the magazine that had fallen open at a double spread. 'Shinty went well?' he managed to ask.

Daniel angled his head and nodded briefly as an answer. 'Now ... if you don't mind ...'

'Yes ... Right then.'

When the footfalls on the staircase had faded to silence Daniel maximised the tab on his laptop he'd hastily minimised on hearing his father's approach.

He returned to reading through the new message that had come in from Ellie.

'I wish you could see me in my new gear,' she'd written. *'You might not be too ashamed to call me your sister.'*

Daniel wished, too, that he could see her in her interview outfit. And did she really think he might be ashamed of her? Had he really given her that impression? That he was some stuck-up geek with a church minister for a dad?

He didn't know what to say in reply so he closed down his laptop and put it in his desk drawer, wishing he had a key to lock it.

Daniel didn't want to stay in the house after supper. The house was never noisy but this evening it seemed intensely quiet. There weren't even any birds to be heard through the open windows. It was cooler now the sun had dipped below the hills and he reckoned he could manage a stroll into the village.

A gang of younger kids was gathered behind the primary school. Daniel recognised their furtive moves as a concealed bottle was passed amongst them. He kept enough distance to avoid the need for communication but they barely spared him a glance as he walked towards the community woodland. Sitting on a bench he took out his mobile. A tawny owl hooted behind him. He decided to leave talking to Alex to the morning—always supposing that after their argument Alex would wait for him to go to school. He hated the thought of a rift between them and wished there'd been a different way to say what had needed saying.

He scrolled down his phone until he reached Caitlin's number. She'd given it to him so they could arrange a meet up to go over the next lot of physics homework. But there was no physics due. Could he just call her for a chat? Or send a text?

As he walked back up the path to the Manse he couldn't tell if the siren he heard was from the fire engine, the police car or the ambulance. He wasn't going to let it spook him—although a call-out for the local emergency services usually meant his father would be called out soon too.

For the second time that evening Caitlin pushed her physics jotter across her desk as she heard her phone give a message-received bleep. She leaned back in her desk chair and swiped her fingers over the screen.

It was a text from Da niel: 'See you tomorrow?'

Caitlin knew they didn't have any classes together on a Friday but she checked her timetable anyway. And what was with the question mark? Text messages could be so difficult to interpret.

Her decision made, she texted back: 'OK. Mum has a meeting in village at 7. Meet at shop?'

It was a couple of minutes before his reply came in: 'Cool. See you then.'

Did she need to answer that? She decided not.

FRIDAY

CHAPTER 13

Early morning had to be the best time ever. Alex lay with his stomach on the springy turf and considered the cove below.

He hadn't wanted to scatter Dad's ashes on the sea but Mum reckoned Dad should be in the place he loved best. How could Alex argue? They'd paddled through the outgoing tide, Mum carrying the casket. An otter, disturbed from its foraging along the shore, viewed them warily as Mum emptied out the ashes. But really? Would Dad have wanted to be in the place where he'd lost everything? Even his catch had been left to rot, with the seagulls fighting over it, before Alex had retrieved and buried it the next day.

Yet Alex was grateful, now, because it was in this spot—the highest point on the clifftops, giving him the widest view of the sea—that he could talk to Dad.

Dad wasn't very good at coming back with helpful answers though. It hadn't been his strongest attribute when he'd been alive, so Alex could hardly complain at the lack of advice now.

'This was where it started. You remember when I told you about him, Dad?' He lifted his chin off his interlocked fingers to scan the view.

It had been during one of these early morning conversations when Alex had first set eyes on Chuck. Even at a distance, and in the misty morning light, Alex could tell the figure rounding the headland wasn't a local. The lad leaving his footprints in the wet sand was dressed in combat trousers and a khaki t-shirt, twirling a stick to flick away strands of seaweed that dared to lie across his path. Alex watched him progress along the beach until he disappeared out of view among a clutch of oak trees growing close to the shore.

Then a few days later when Alex had been at the cove, busy sanding down his boat in preparation for repainting, he'd been caught by surprise.

'Need any help?'

Alex swung around to see the stranger a few metres away. 'No,' he said and turned back to carry on with his task.

If Alex thought that was an end to the conversation he'd been very wrong.

'I could work on the other side. Here, pass me a bit of sandpaper.'

'No. Really. I'm fine.'

But Alex could feel the lad continue to watch him smooth the curves of the wooden boards.

'I'm Chuck, by the way.' He gave a mid-Atlantic twang on the name, but Alex could hear a close-to-Glasgow accent on the rest of his words.

'You're supposed to tell me your name now,' Chuck continued.

'Alex,' Alex said, keeping his eyes firmly on his task.

'Thought I'd go for a swim. You want to come, Alex?'

By the time Alex did look at him, Chuck had taken off his t-shirt and was unzipping his combat trousers.

'What do you think about me then?' Chuck asked.

Alex frowned, confused.

'You know. First impressions?' Chuck flung his t-shirt and trousers on the rocks and tightened the cord in the swimming shorts he was wearing.

Alex liked words but there was no luxury of debate here. Chuck stood waiting for his answer. 'Cocky,' Alex's brain supplied and it came out of his mouth without censure.

Chuck repeated the word as if trying it on for size. And from his expression, and the way he held his limbs, he seemed happy with the fit.

'Come on then. What're you waiting for?'

Alex gave the lad a sideways glance then took off his t-shirt and jeans, folding them before dropping them in the boat. He tightened the cord in his own swimming shorts and followed Chuck down the beach.

'Swim out to that rock?'

'All right,' Alex said. 'But it's called a skerry by the way.'

'Whatever.'

They ran together down the beach and through the shallows. Alex loved the bite of the water as it splashed his thighs. The other boy didn't flinch against the sudden cold either. He was a strong swimmer too, and as they launched themselves into the deeper water he made the headway.

Alex knew the waters around here. Of course he did. He could get to the skerry with his eyes closed, even with the strong undercurrent on the shore side. Alex turned over and swam back crawl for a few moments but when he turned over again Chuck was nowhere to be seen. Alex plunged beneath the surface and could see Chuck swimming underwater, still up ahead. He would soon be in the undercurrent and could easily be taken off course.

Alex came back up to the surface and called out Chuck's name. When he saw his head bob up he shouted, 'Keep to your left.'

Chuck raised an arm in understanding before he dived under again. And after a couple more minutes, Alex saw Chuck hauling himself onto the jagged rocks of the skerry as two disgruntled seals slid off.

When Alex pulled himself onto the rock Chuck was already flat on his back, his arms spread wide, his chest rising and falling with his deep breaths.

'And now,' Chuck said with his eyes closed against the noon-high sun, 'because I won, you have to suck my big toe.' With his eyes still firmly closed, he raised his left leg and waggled his toes.

Alex felt the saw-toothed rocks sting the soles of his feet.

Chuck eventually lifted his head and looked at him. 'Ha ha. Your face,' he said, laughing out loud. 'I wouldn't ask you to do that.'

Alex relaxed slightly.

'Not yet. We've only just met.' And on that final word, Chuck had given him a wink.

Alex hadn't given any serious thought about that day before now. Too much had gone on since. But reliving it all again made him realise how easily he'd been manipulated. Chuck offering to help sand his boat, when really he wanted Alex to help *him*. Asking Alex all about himself as they relaxed on the skerry before swimming back to shore, when really Chuck was only waiting to tell his own story—drip by drip, leaving Alex eager to see him again for the next instalment. That his yarns were difficult to believe didn't seem to matter back then. Whether his dad really was in witness protection. Or if his mother, who Chuck clearly idolised and was concerned about, was really so dependent on him?

He'd been sucked in by Chuck's crazy conversations too. Who else had ever asked him, 'What is it that you long for, Alex? What do you most want out of life?' Chuck had made him feel somehow ... raw ... yet more alive, too, as if his own thick outer skin was being sandpapered off.

But that was all in the past now.

There was no chance of ever forgetting Chuck—and Alex would never know if Chuck's stories were true—but at least he wasn't around to torment him anymore.

Dragging his thoughts to the day ahead, Alex stood up and gave a final wave to Dad. The telephone bill scrunched in his jeans pocket. 'Chuck's the least of my problems now, heh?'

True to form, Dad kept his opinion to himself.

Back at the house Alex pushed aside a mewing moggy from the door, knowing he had plenty of time before Mum got up. He'd be in the kitchen, doling out her porridge—the only food she could face in the morning, whatever the weather—when she came downstairs, stretching her arms above her head to ease the ache in her back.

He took the telephone bill out of his pocket and stuffed it at the back of a kitchen drawer before measuring out the oats, water and milk into the pan.

Quarter of an hour later Alex took out his battered phone, checked his credit and texted Moth: Be at the boat in 15.

No point going to school on a Friday. The weather being the way it was, it could be a busy night in the hotel. Tony would be grateful for a few extras.

CHAPTER 14

Five more minutes, Alex decided. If Moth hadn't turned up in the next five minutes he'd leave without her. He'd already checked the boat over and stowed a couple of apples from the garden along with the sandwiches he'd made for them both in the locker beneath his seat.

He checked his phone again: 9:20am. That was it. He untied the painter from its iron ring and started to push the boat along the beach.

'Hey.'

Alex turned to the cliffs. Moth was clambering over the edge, holding on to wind stunted bushes as she started her way down the slope.

'Wait for me.'

Alex feigned annoyance when she eventually reached him but he was pleased she'd made it, for the distraction of her company as much as for the help she had already proved she could be.

'I like that t-shirt,' Moth said, perching on the gunwale and swinging her legs in the boat. 'It makes you look sexy.'

Alex pushed the boat into the water.

'And the way you wear it—rolled up sleeves. Shows off your bulging biceps.'

'Leave it.'

'When did Mr Let's Have Fun turn into Mr Grumpy?'

'I said—'

'I know. You don't need to go on.' Moth settled into what had become her favourite position, nestled amongst the ropes.

Alex fought against a north wind as he pulled clear of the cove.

'Keeps you fit, rowing, doesn't it?' Moth continued, seemingly oblivious to Alex's reluctance for conversation. 'Don't know why you want to get a motor.'

'You know very well that a motor will let me do more than just empty a few creels.' And although Moth's body language suggested she'd heard enough—in fact heard it all before, thank you very much—he went on. 'So that fat tourists with more money than sense can gorge themselves on what I bring to them. I want a motor so that when I can afford diving equipment—'

'Diving equipment your mother has sworn she'll never let you use.'

'... So that when I can afford diving equipment I'll be able to bring a wider variety of shellfish to a greater number of discerning obese tourists.'

'Glad I asked.'

'And get paid more for my efforts.'

Alex continued rowing through the ensuing silence until he reached his first buoy. Hauling the creel from the slate grey water, he was disappointed to find it empty. The catch from the next was only marginally better. He swithered about whether the small crab in there was worth keeping.

As Alex reset the creels, Moth stood up to swap positions. 'I'll row for a bit,' she offered.

Alex shrugged his reply, lowering the creels until they were out of sight.

With her back to the horizon, Moth pulled on the oars. 'She'd be all right, you know,' she said, her eyes fixed on Alex. 'Without you.'

There was no point in pretending he didn't know what Moth was on about. 'No she wouldn't. She makes barely any money from those rag dolls she insists on trying to flog at all the crazy craft markets she has to drive miles to get to. She has no idea how much cash I put in the housekeeping tin. Never mind the bills.'

'But she's been so much better this summer.'

'Oh yes. Better in that she doesn't wander around the village any more, wildly shouting for Dad.' Alex knew his duty and wasn't going to shirk it. 'She has a long way to go yet … She needs me, all right. And what I can earn by doing this.'

It was well into the afternoon before Alex called it a day. The catch was little more than he normally took in a few hours. Still, he could get it to the hotel before they started preparing the evening dinner. He couldn't fault Moth either. She'd pulled her weight all right.

'I'll see how much I can get out of Tony,' he said. 'I can let you have something for helping out.'

'No need. Payment enough getting to spend quality time with you.'

Was she being sarcastic? Watching her tuck herself up for a sleep he decided not. He took the oars and headed towards the shore.

They were in sight of the village when he woke her.

'You want me to drop you off before I go to the hotel?' he said as she blinked opened her eyes.

'What? No, it's okay. I'll stick with you.' She wrestled herself into a sitting position and scanned the shore. 'Shit. What day is it?'

Alex laughed at her. 'Friday. All day.'

'Shit,' she said again. 'Probation Officer. Half four.' She looked at her phone. 'She won't mind if I'm a bit late.'

'Christ, Moth. Get the other oar. We'll be quicker together.'

Alex shuffled along the wooden seat to make room for her. But as she stood, Moth's left leg buckled at the knee.

'Shit on a bike,' she said, standing on one leg. She dropped her phone and clasped her hands around the leg that had obviously gone numb.

The boat rocked from side to side. Alex stood up carefully to reach out for her but one moment she was there, wobbling about, and the next she had overbalanced and was in the water. Alex straddled the boat to maintain his balance as it tipped sideways. Moth was completely out of sight. The water had folded over her with the rolling of a wave.

Alex threw the oars in the boat, scrabbled out of his trainers and plunged in after her. Diving below the surface he could see Moth quite close to him, curled in a ball. With two strong strokes he was able to reach out and grab the back of her sweater. He managed to slide an arm around her waist and use his free arm to get them both back to the surface. With her head out of the water now, Moth coughed and spluttered. Water streamed out of her nose.

Struggling to keep his own head above the water, Alex could see the boat drifting back towards the shore. He turned on his back and cupped his hand around Moth's chin, the way he'd been taught.

'Relax,' he shouted at her and her body straightened out above his own as he kicked his legs madly to reach the boat. He caught hold of the rowlock and manoeuvred them both into a position where Moth could grab the gunwale. And although the boat tilted and started filling with water as they hauled themselves in, eventually they were both safe.

Within a few minutes of her falling overboard, Moth was lying on her side on the wooden deck, hugging her knees and complaining.

CHAPTER 15

Tony—mug in one hand, cigarette in the other—was sitting on a small stool outside the kitchen door when Alex made his way to the rear entrance of the hotel. After pulling a last drag from the cigarette Tony stubbed it out on the gravel path and pocketed the tab before giving Alex a wave.

'I reckon you've put a spell on this weather. We're booked up all weekend,' Tony said emptying the remains of his coffee on the flowerbed. 'Come on in. Let's see what you've got for me.'

Alex followed him into the kitchen. Along three walls were a range of stainless steel units and shelving and two huge fridges. On the other wall, a window gave a view over the kitchen garden where Tony grew his salad greens. Along the outside windowsill was a line of seashells: scallops, oysters, a prize conch. A fat ginger cat sat in the corner of the window, looking in. Most of the food preparation was done on a worktop below this window.

Tony gave his mug a rinse and topped it up with more coffee from a filter machine before lifting the lid on the box which Alex still had in both hands. He gave an appraising glance over the contents: 'Thirty-five?'

Alex felt himself blush. No way was the catch worth that much but Tony had stuck out his hand to seal the deal.

'Something wrong?' Tony said.

Alex shrugged his shoulders. There was no way he could turn the offer down. 'Maybe it's a bit too much?' he said.

'End of the month bonus included.'

Alex wasn't going to argue anymore. He put the box on the worktop, took Tony's hand and shook on it.

'It's going to be a long weekend with all these visitors. What're you up to?' Tony asked.

'Shinty league match tomorrow,' Alex said without really considering Tony's words.

'Oh well,' Tony said, 'another time. Get yourself a coffee,' he continued, disappearing into his small office.

What was Tony suggesting? If he needed help around the hotel Alex could do that. But the chance had gone for now.

Alex half-filled a mug with the thick brown liquid and took a long drink. On the shelves next to the coffee machine were boxes of foodstuff. Alex picked up an individual portion jar of jam: strawberry. He felt his neck redden. Just two weeks ago he'd been scanning these same shelves wondering if he could lift anything to take to Chuck. Tony came out of the office and Alex quickly dropped the jam jar back in the box.

'You can take a couple if you want,' Tony said. 'For your mother.'

'Oh. No thanks. I made some rhubarb and ginger. She likes that.'

'Hmm. Sounds good.'

'Maybe I ...' An idea had flashed through Alex's head. But the stupidity of the idea followed just as quickly.

'Spill the beans.'

'I was going to say I could provide you with some homemade jam but realised how ridiculous that would be when you can make your own.'

Tony gave him a lopsided grin. 'Not ridiculous at all ... I don't have time. Bring me some samples—fancy flavours—and we'll see how they go down.'

'Oh. Right.'

Tony disappeared into his office again and returned with two fivers. 'You'll need ingredients.'

CHAPTER 16

At the end of the hotel driveway Alex fanned the notes in his hand to count them again before stuffing them in his pocket. He met Moth on the road where he'd left her to make her call. She looked younger in his old school sweater and joggers. He kept them as spare clothes in his boat and Moth had gratefully changed into them when they'd got back to shore. His own sodden jeans were clinging to his legs but his t-shirt had already dried on him.

'I owe you big time,' Moth said, pocketing her phone.

'Was she understanding?'

Moth went into a long story of how she'd explained to her Probation Officer all about her accident and how she'd been valiantly rescued. Alex couldn't tell if Moth was taking the piss.

'She was especially impressed that I'd been helping out a friend.' Moth punched Alex on the arm. 'But, you know, I could've probably made it to the boat myself when I'd got the feeling back in my leg,' she said as they set off towards to the village centre.

'You what!'

'Relax. You are now my official hero.'

Alex did relax a little, his walk becoming as close to a swagger as he could manage.

'For today, anyway,' Moth added.

She led him into the shop where they stood side by side in front of the soft drinks. A couple of blokes from the fish farm stood near to them, contemplating the shelves of booze.

'Give us a twenty,' Moth said to Alex, the words coming out of the side of her mouth with a hiss.

Alex stood rock still.

'Just a loan. Quick!'

Alex pulled out the money Tony had given him and passed over a twenty. Moth palmed it and sidled towards the fish farm blokes.

With her back to the close circuit camera that was aimed at the booze shelves, Moth opened her hand to show the note.

'Vodka. Litre.'

'Piss off.'

'You can keep the change.'

That swayed it. Without looking around, the nearest bloke took the cash off her, added a litre bottle of vodka to his wire basket and made his way to the checkout. They queued behind him with their bottle of orange squash.

Outside the shop there was no chance of the blokes forgetting to pass the bottle over. Moth was as close behind them as a girl with a litre of vodka to lose could be.

The transaction completed, and the vodka safely stashed in her bag, Moth turned to head to the wooden chalet in the woods where she lived with her mum and Moth's middle-aged brother.

'Beach tonight,' she said. 'I'll text you.'

Wondering how it had cost him twenty pounds to be a hero, Alex made his way to the pier to take his boat back to her mooring in the cove.

Mum was on the sofa when Alex got home, watching losers on the telly trying to win an amount of money that would be only a fraction of the amount the idiot presenter would earn from that one show.

'They're doing it for charity,' Mum said in reply to Alex's disparaging comment.

He went through to the kitchen. Using his thumbnail, he chipped stuck-on porridge from Mum's breakfast bowl in the sink. She'd had a tin of tomato soup for her lunch. Well, half of one. The congealed remaining half was still in the tin on the windowsill. Alex checked the fridge.

'You didn't eat your sandwich,' he called through to the living room.

'I've gone off beef spread.'

Great. Another thing to add to the ham, tinned fish and egg that she'd "gone off".

'You can't have peanut butter every day,' he said, trying to hide the irritation he felt.

'Oh, I'm fine. I had a banana.'

Alex looked in the fruit bowl. There had been two bananas there this morning. There were two now. 'I think that might have been the other day, Mum.'

'If you say so.' She sounded more than tired. Alex wasn't sure which was worse: Mum frantically trying to get her latest craft project together for the markets, or Mum lying on the sofa, watching telly and forgetting to eat.

Alex placed the palms of his hands against either side of the kitchen door frame and peered through to the living room. 'Want another cuppa?' he asked.

'I'm a bit done in,' Mum said, sliding her feet into her furry slippers. 'I must have caught a bug at the market. I'll go for a lie down.'

'I'll call you when tea's ready.' He knew better than to ask if she fancied the spaghetti Neopolitana he'd planned. He would plate up a small portion for her and hope she'd eat at least some of it. Getting the ingredients together, he chose the ripest tomatoes that he'd fetched in from the polytunnel, wishing he'd kept back a couple of the langoustines he'd caught to go with it for her.

His mobile buzzing on the kitchen windowsill woke him. He'd fallen asleep at the kitchen table—his head on his outstretched arms. He picked up his tomato sauce smeared plate and slid it into the now cold washing-up water in the sink, then rinsed his glass before placing it upside down on the drainer.

Mum's tea was still on the kitchen worktop despite him calling her several times. The basil leaf he'd put on top had wilted. He very nearly tipped the food in the bin, but knew they couldn't afford such drama queen behaviour. Instead he covered it with another plate and put it in the fridge, then checked his phone. 'Get down here,' Moth had texted. 'Pre-party drinks at the pier.'

He didn't go up to see Mum but wrote her a quick note saying where he was going. Pre-party drinks suddenly seemed like a good idea—after he'd shut up the hens for the night, that is.

CHAPTER 17

Caitlin had spent most of the day in the biology lab researching for her practical investigation. Fascinated by an article on cyber-psychology and gaming, she was considering how she might conduct a school-based experiment to produce any significant findings. Her earlier forays on Google Scholar into the effects of gaming on teenagers had enraged her, with the majority of the papers on offer highlighting the negatives. And okay, maybe she wasn't going to discover that battling evil online was upping teenagers' moral compasses, but she was hopeful she could undertake a small-scale study where some of the advantages of gaming were centre stage.

So when she met Daniel outside the shop that evening it was the first time she'd seen him all day. Something in the middle of her chest gave a quick flip as he approached her with his, for once, well-groomed hair.

She happily agreed with Daniel's suggestion that they walk up to the Old Manse, and within five minutes they were out of the village, climbing *Druim na Muice*, the hill with its Gaelic name meaning pig's ridge.

They followed a burn, which had quickly returned to being not much more than a trickle after the storm waters had flooded through. As they climbed in single file along the narrow path, the water burbling beside them, Caitlin noticed Daniel was still limping.

'You shinty players. You're always getting injured, aren't you?'

She regretted the question when Daniel spun around with a barely concealed scowl. 'Sorry. I didn't mean to...'

'No. I'm sorry,' Daniel said quickly. His hand made a tentative move towards her wrist.

But Caitlin took a half-step backwards and Daniel's hand dropped to his side.

After a brief awkward silence, they started off again.

She followed a few paces behind him until they reached the brow of a hill where the church and the derelict Old Manse loomed ahead of them. 'Is this where you used to live then? In the Old Manse?'

But Daniel had spoken at the same time as her and she only caught the end of his question: '... your dad?' he'd said.

'Sorry. After you,' Daniel said.

Caitlin shrugged. 'It wasn't important.'

She responded to his nervous laugh with a nervous laugh of her own before they carried on walking side by side towards the church. When they reached a bench that overlooked the graveyard Daniel sat down heavily then shuffled to one end to make more room. Caitlin sat beside him.

'I was just asking how your mum and dad are,' Daniel said as he swivelled on the bench to face her. 'It was good meeting them the other night.'

'Yeah. They're fine. Mum said you can come anytime. She thought you were very polite.'

'Right.'

'Believe me ... it's a compliment from her.' She watched Daniel stretch his bad leg out in front of him but she wasn't going to make the same mistake of commenting on it again.

Daniel's head drooped until he was staring at his feet. 'She might not say that if she knew me better.'

'What's that supposed to mean?' The words were out before she could stop them. Why couldn't she control her tongue?

'I'm sorry ... Ignore me. I'm an idiot,' Daniel said, still apparently talking to his trainers.

'I wouldn't have come just to ignore you,' she said but Daniel gave no indication of having heard her.

They sat in silence for a longer time than she was happy with.

Thankfully it was Daniel who spoke first. 'Eva gave me some scones for us,' he said, lifting his head to face her at last.

Glad of the distraction, Caitlin took a buttered scone from the plastic tub Daniel fished out of his backpack.

'Hmm. Jam as well,' she said, opening up the two halves of scone. 'I can never understand why people feel they can only have either butter or jam.'

Daniel gave a brief 'huh'. He obviously wasn't interested in her opinion on scones. Fair enough. She would finish their impromptu picnic then get back to the village as soon as possible. This was verging on the painful.

But was she being too hasty? As she bit into her scone she thought back to their first meeting. Daniel had been kind and considerate. And he'd told her about his mum.

God, she was thick. They were only sitting overlooking the graveyard where his mum would be buried.

With their silence reinstated, Caitlin was surprised when Daniel spoke again, mid-mouthful. 'You're so pretty,' he said.

Well that's what it sounded like. Had she heard him right? Could he have said something else, something other than pretty? His tone of voice had been right for pretty.

She swallowed her mouthful with difficulty, the claggy mixture sticking to her tongue and the back of her mouth. 'Sorry?'

And now he'd gone bright red and she was asking him to repeat what he'd said.

'I think you're really pretty.'

'Thank you.' She stretched her hand along the bench and allowed a fragment of hope to establish itself. She looked at his sad face and the bit of scone caught in the corner of his mouth. 'You're not unattractive yourself.'

As he smiled, the bit of scone dropped from his mouth onto his hand. He quickly rubbed his face and wiped his hand down his trouser leg.

Caitlin smiled back.

When they'd both finished eating and had shared a bottle of water Caitlin got up to wander around the graveyard. It was well kept, the grass mown, the hedges trimmed, just like the rest of the grounds surrounding the church.

The garden of the Old Manse was a different matter. It was almost as if the shrubs and trees were trying to hide the dark, square-built house.

Daniel came and stood beside her. 'It never seemed so gloomy when I was a kid,' he said.

'Why doesn't the church sell it?' Caitlin wanted to know.

'Nobody wants to buy it.'

'Can't say I'm surprised.' It was as if the place had given up on the fight for life.

'Come on though,' Daniel said, holding out his hand. And when she took it, he led her to a path that wound behind the church. 'I think you'll like this.'

The path gradually dropped down a rise and, still holding hands, they passed through a group of lime trees buzzing with bees. They stepped out from the shade of the trees into slanting sunbeams and Daniel pulled on Caitlin's hand to stop her in her tracks. It was a moment before she realised the vast expanse of green in front of them was actually a lochan. At the far edge she could see water lilies but just a couple of steps ahead of her the lochan was covered by a mat of waterweeds. A few twigs shaken off the trees by the recent storm drifted in slight currents.

Daniel guided her around the edge of the lochan until they came to a wooden-slatted pier sticking out across the water.

'We used to sit here for ages watching for newts ... Alex and me.' He hesitated and Caitlin sensed he had more to say. 'God. Things were so simple back then.'

'I can just imagine the pair of you. Both in green wellies, I bet.'

Daniel laughed. 'Yep. And cut-off trackies for shorts. Come on,' he said, twitching her hand and stepping onto the pier.

'Is it safe?' The slats were flaking away at the edges. The wood looked rotten and soft.

'Only one way to find out.' Daniel grinned at her and sidled on. Caitlin followed along until they got to the end and they stood side by side, their toes poking over the edge. The dense lily pads, with their mass of white flowers, made the surface look solid.

'How deep is it?' Caitlin asked.

'Only one way to find out,' Daniel said again and stuck out a foot as if he was about to step off the pier.

'Don't!' Caitlin lashed out a hand to grab his shirt but Daniel swivelled around to face her, grinning even wider.

Caitlin let go of his shirt, but she left her hand on the small of his back. Daniel slid an arm around her waist. There was a question in his eyes. She let him come closer and kiss her.

With arms wrapped around each other's backs they took their time on their return to the village, stopping every now and then to share things about themselves with each other: the new bands they'd recently discovered, the films and videogames they enjoyed, their favourite pizza toppings.

When they reached the burn they both balanced on a large rock and watched the sun gradually sinking towards the sea. The sounds of a beach party filtered towards them through the tall grasses.

'No more news on the girl that drowned, is there?' Caitlin asked.

'Girl?' Daniel said and stepped off the rock.

'You know ... She was found near Alex's boat.'

'It wasn't a girl.'

'It was when Constable Logan called yesterday to ask if I'd seen any girls I didn't recognise around the area recently.' Caitlin too stepped off the rock.

But she didn't know how to answer when Daniel grabbed his hair in his hands and said, 'Oh God. What the fuck?'

CHAPTER 18

Walking through the village, Alex let himself unwind a little. Mum would be all right for the evening. And he *had* saved Moth from drowning. He deserved a bit of a let-up.

Some of his composure disappeared as he approached the turnoff for the Manse. He hadn't been in contact with Daniel all day. But then again, he reasoned, Daniel hadn't bothered to text him either. It was always Alex who had to make the effort, going to the Manse after tea ... making sure he was on the road in time to meet Daniel in the morning. And let's face it, he thought, Daniel had well and truly dismissed him last night.

Alex's justifications for the lack of contact between them got him to the other side of the village, where he heard bass beats booming even before he turned on to the track to the pier. Walking towards the pier, Alex could see at least thirty teenagers ranged on the slipway and along the stony beach on both sides—hangers-on staying overnight because of the party swelling the local population.

Alex had a bad feeling. The warm weather, open drinking amongst the younger kids—the new constable would be out soon enough with this amount of noise.

Moth spotted him and ran over, flinging her arms around his neck, the vodka bottle in her hand nearly braining him. She slipped a warm hand into his and led him to the group she'd just broken away from. Alex knew them all, but they were mainly from Moth's old class at school.

A couple of years back, at a party like this, somebody would have brought along a guitar and there'd be old Fleetwood Mac songs to sing along to. Back then, with cheap cider and maybe a bottle of fizzy wine to get them as far off their faces as they wanted to get, their quick gropes in the sand dunes were of no more significance than puppies tumbling together.

Now the progression to vodka and a collective history of experimental screws, some more satisfactory than others, made for a different tone of party.

A few folk got up to dance, girls flinging their arms, the boys going for a more pogoing style in an attempt to keep with the beat.

Alex found a plastic beaker and let Moth tip in a slug of vodka with a splash of orange squash. He propped himself against the pier wall and necked the drink, feeling the warmth from stones that had been in the sun all day on his back and the heat from the vodka in his gut.

He didn't move from his spot. There was no need. He slipped further and further down the wall until his legs stretched out in front of him and his arms fell limp at his sides—Moth visiting him every so often to replenish his plastic beaker.

He knew he'd had enough to drink when he saw Chuck walking along the clifftop opposite. Not only was Chuck dead, but no way would he let himself be seen in the open like that.

Alex let his head flop back against the wall and shut his eyes. He wasn't planning on opening them for quite some time.

* * *

Daniel couldn't remember ever feeling so happy. Sitting in the back seat of Caitlin's parents' car he reached out and touched Caitlin's hand, which she'd snaked around the back of the passenger seat. It was as if an electric shock passed through him and he scrunched his toes in his trainers.

'Thanks for the lift,' he said hopping out of the car when Caitlin's mum came to a halt outside the Manse.

He really wanted to feel Caitlin's lips on his own again before going indoors but Caitlin stayed put in the car, giving him a little wave as the car pulled away. It wasn't long before he knew she felt the same. No sooner had he drifted upstairs to his bedroom his phone beeped with a text from her. It gave him another bolt of pleasure as he read it.

He wasn't quite so sure how he felt about the news of Chuck though. Somewhere, Chuck was very much alive. He'd tried phoning Alex as soon as Caitlin had dropped her bombshell, but the call hadn't got through.

As he sat at his desk and opened his laptop he tried calling him again. 'This number is currently unavailable,' the mechanical voice repeated. He sent a text: 'Big news. Phone me as soon as you get this.'

While he waited for his email account on his laptop to open, he composed a reply to Caitlin's text. Then clicking on his Inbox, he saw that a new message from Ellie had come in.

SATURDAY

CHAPTER 19

Daniel rolled on to his good side and grabbed his phone: 5:50am. The sun was already providing enough light to see clearly in his bedroom. Not that it would have mattered if he'd switched on all the lights and stomped around making as much noise as he could. His father was away by now. It was probably the noise of the car leaving that had woken him.

Under the comfort of his duvet, he explored the edges of the blister behind his knee with his fingertips. It was less sore to touch now. Probably the antibiotics fighting off the infection. The doctor had said it wouldn't take long for him to notice a difference.

He sat up in bed, took another antibiotic with a sip of water and opened his laptop. He hadn't changed his mind overnight. He was going to meet Ellie. Today. Why shouldn't he?

He read again their email exchange from last night. She'd been the one to suggest a meet up. And although Daniel would normally have preferred to get his head around such a momentous event before committing, he'd got caught up with Ellie's exuberance and agreed. Within a few messages it was all arranged, Ellie suggesting Perth. She could get a bus there easily enough and she knew where there was a park where they could walk. And as it was a Saturday, she normally went out in the afternoon, so she wouldn't have to say anything about it to her foster family.

Daniel couldn't remember a time when he hadn't known he was adopted. His parents had never made a big deal about it—he'd never been referred to as 'special' or 'chosen'. But he knew his experiences had been a whole lot different to Ellie's.

His plans were clear. Get the first bus from the village to town. Then there were plenty of buses to Perth—he'd looked up the timetable—they ran almost every hour. He could spend time with Ellie, just an hour or so in neutral territory, before they both got their own buses back home. Nobody would know they were meeting up, and if it didn't work out too well there were fewer people involved. But he hoped it would go well, that they would become friends.

It was weird—although he'd always known their birth mother had chosen to keep Ellie and let Daniel go for adoption he didn't feel any resentment towards Ellie, especially knowing how it had worked out for them both. And on the one occasion in his early teens when he had thrown a wobbler complaining about his birth mother just 'giving him away', his father had reminded him not to judge anybody *until you've walked a mile in their shoes.*

Even back then Daniel had known it wasn't just a platitude—it was how his father lived his own life. And Daniel was proud of him for it.

Daniel still hadn't sent Ellie a picture of himself and she hadn't sent any either. But they'd arranged a spot to meet on Google Earth. There wouldn't be many girls standing next to the statue of John Knox at 1:25pm.

When Alex next opened his eyes he could make out a pinewood-framed window and flowery curtains. Not his own bed then. He swivelled his eyes to take in as much of the room as he could, not sure his head was up to movement just yet. Moth's jacket was hanging on a cupboard handle. He was in Moth's narrow bed. It had been a couple of years since he'd slept there.

Hearing voices coming from the kitchen through the chalet's thin walls, Alex rolled out of bed and pulled on his t-shirt and jeans, which had been discarded on the bedroom floor. A glass of orange juice was balanced on a stool next to the bed. For him? It was thick against his tongue and the acid caught the back of his throat. When he'd decided it was going to stay in his stomach he ventured into the kitchen.

'Aunty Joan. Stewart,' he said, nodding in turn to each of the two people sitting at the table. Stewart had the local newspaper spread out. It looked as if he'd been reading out items of interest to Aunty Joan while she flicked through her phone. With a page-a-day diary open in front of her, she was pencilling in appointments.

'Well, I've seen worse,' Aunty Joan said, glancing at Alex.

Alex mumbled a reply. He needed to get on. He found his jacket hanging on the pegs by the door and fished his mobile out of his pocket. The battery was completely dead.

'Don't worry. I phoned your mother a while back. She knows you're here.'

'Oh. Thanks.'

Alex looked up at the wall clock. 'Fuck,' he said and then blanched at his slip.

Aunty Joan picked up her breakfast dishes and moved to the sink, tutting.

'You need to be somewhere?' Stewart asked.

'Yeah. Shinty match. I need to get my gear.'

'I'll give you a run down.'

'It's all right ... you don't have—'

'I've got to call at the shop anyway. I'll get my keys. See you outside.' With that, Stewart disappeared into his bedroom.

'Thanks, Aunty Joan.' He put on his trainers that had been placed neatly by somebody, obviously not him, beside the door.

'Any time,' she said, without turning around.

Alex peered into the living room area that was really just another section off the kitchen. Moth was flat out on the sofa, her mouth hanging open. He could have ended up anywhere. She'd looked out for him.

Stewart swung the Nissan into the croft driveway and Alex saw Mum walking away from the house carrying a plastic tub of scraps towards the hen coop. She took long strides in her black wellies; her hair, with its coppery tints, glossy this morning. She stopped and put down the tub as the Nissan pulled up. Stewart cut the engine and jumped out.

'Quick as you can,' Stewart called as Alex gave a quick wave to mum and ran towards the house.

In his bedroom Alex quickly stuffed his shinty gear in his backpack and headed out again.

When he got back outside, Stewart had an arm around Mum's shoulders and her head was resting on his shoulder. It was a friendly gesture—nothing inappropriate—still ...

Stewart got back in the car and started the engine.

'What time's the match?' Mum asked Alex as he opened the passenger door. 'I might come and watch.'

'Two o'clock ... but—'

'Great—'

'But it's an away match.'

Mum's smile drooped. 'Oh. Right. Good luck then.' She squeezed his arm and gave him a peck on the cheek.

And as Stewart revved the recalcitrant engine Alex watched his mum pick up the tub of scraps and set out again on her way to feed the hens. Stewart turned and gave him a brief smile as he coaxed the sputtering vehicle onto the single-track road. Alex knew he wouldn't have made it to the team bus in time this morning if it hadn't been for Stewart. So why did he feel so ungrateful to him?

Daniel sprinted the last fifty metres to the bus stop even though he knew he was in good time. Sure enough, he was the first person there. He perched on the thin rail in the bus shelter and checked the wall behind him didn't have anything revolting smeared across it before leaning back. A few minutes later a couple from the village joined him. After a nod of the head from the bloke and a 'How are you, Daniel?' from the old biddy, they went on with their own discussions. Nobody would think it unusual for him to be waiting for the bus; the only unusual thing was that he was on his own. Not with Alex.

The bus took about forty minutes to get to town and the first two miles of the road was single-track. Every now and then the bus jolted Daniel out of his thoughts as it pulled into a passing place to allow tourists with their cars rammed full of luggage to navigate the road.

The view out of the window was the same as ever. Daniel knew that on his way home the view would be the same too. It would be him that would be different. He would have met his twin sister.

He might even have found out more about why they'd been separated when they were babies, seeing as Ellie had lived with their birth mother for the first few years of her life. But he'd got that information from his father, not from Ellie. And Ellie might not even remember her. Daniel had told himself that at this first meeting he wouldn't pry. He would keep it simple, nothing heavy. Day-to-day stuff only. She had told him a bit about the foster family she was with at the moment. That was enough to be going on with.

Not wanting to draw attention to himself as the bus pulled into the station he let the other passengers go first. He muttered a thanks to the driver and stepped off the bus. The High Street up ahead looked busy and as everybody scuttled towards the shops and the bus pulled away, he was left standing alone at the bus stance. Forty minutes before the Perth bus left—he had time to get a coke in the train station café. He crossed the road and the half-empty car park and entered the long narrow underpass that linked the two stations.

'Daniel.' A voice came from behind him.

Recognising the voice, Daniel swivelled around.

And there he was—at the entrance to the underpass, his diamond earring glinting in the sunlight and that crazy look in his eyes.

Daniel turned and continued down the slope of the underpass. Big mistake. He could hear footsteps behind him. He broke into a run but the footfalls behind him kept pace.

'No need to ignore me, Daniel. We're friends, aren't we?'

It was dark in the tunnel, several of the overhead lights had been smashed in, but the exit wasn't far now. He'd be amongst other people soon enough.

'I can give you a lift if you want. My van is just in the car park.'

But still Daniel didn't turn around. Not until he heard the words: 'I can take you straight to Ellie.'

CHAPTER 20

The bus dropped the team in the village but Alex didn't go to the pub with the others, despite there being a cost-price supper waiting for them. He would get back and cook for Mum. He headed up the road, his shadow stretching ahead of him.

The Nissan was parked by the back door. Stewart wasn't in the habit of calling that often and anyway he'd seen Mum only this morning. Alex quickened his pace. Was something wrong with Mum?

He called out as he entered the back door. Mum's reply came from upstairs and he took the stairs two at a time until he barged right in to Stewart on the landing.

'Mum. Are you all right?' He pushed past Stewart to get to Mum's bedroom. She was standing in the middle of the room holding a t-shirt. Her small holdall was open on the bed. She turned to look at him and he could tell she'd been crying.

'What is it?' He kept his voice as gentle as possible, but Mum just shook her head.

Alex turned to Stewart who was hovering by the door. 'What's happened?'

'Best if you speak to your Aunty Joan. She's downstairs,' Stewart said, standing aside to let Alex go past.

Alex thundered down the stairs and in to the kitchen. Aunty Joan was sitting at the kitchen table, her mobile in her hands. The pages of the phone bill that he'd pushed to the back of the kitchen drawer lay spread across the table.

'What's going on?' Alex demanded. 'That's none of your business.'

Aunty Joan turned and held him with a hard stare. 'It is very much my business when my sister has to walk all the way to my house to get help because her phone has been cut off.'

'They can't do that! I'm paying it.'

'They can, and they have.'

Alex read the section of the page Aunty Joan was pointing to. ...*no outgoing calls until the outstanding amount has been paid in full.* It went on to explain how to get emergency services if needed. He was certain he'd read all the pages carefully. How had he missed that?

'Your mother was distraught when I came back here with her and we found this. All these calls. I would ask what you've been up to—'

'Mum must have—'

'Don't you dare!' Aunty Joan exploded.

'What? What are you talking about?'

'Don't come it. Premium calls. I googled a few of the numbers.'

Despite himself, Alex felt himself blush at her insinuations. 'Really. I haven't—' But there was no way he would be able to convince her it hadn't been him making those calls.

'I'll sort this out on Monday. But don't think you're getting away with it. Cathy's coming to stay with me for a bit.'

'No way!'

Aunty Joan ignored him, getting up and leaving the kitchen.

'No way,' Alex called to her retreating back. He followed her to the door but came to a halt when he saw Mum coming downstairs, and behind her, Stewart carrying her holdall.

'Tell her, Mum,' Alex said as they all trooped outside. 'Tell her we're fine!'

But Stewart was already holding the passenger seat of the Nissan forward so that Mum could get in the back.

'Leave it for now, Alex.' Stewart passed Mum's holdall in to the car. 'She'll be okay with us for a while.'

'How long, though?'

Aunty Joan gave her closing comment on the matter. 'Get the place cleaned up and then we'll see.'

Alex saw red at that. Having a clean house was so important, was it? Who was Aunty Joan to dictate housekeeping rules to them? She might keep the chalet tidy but she was quite happy to dish up ready meals every night. No way would that do for Mum. Alex stood fuming as the Nissan left the croft.

He gathered up the pages of the phone bill and pushed them back in the envelope. Why hadn't *he* thought about checking those numbers? It was obviously an error somehow. No way was he going to let Aunty Joan get involved with this. It was his problem and he would sort it out. And before Monday.

He realised he was starving. Not having time to make himself a packed lunch this morning, he'd not eaten all day. The two bananas in the fruit bowl were brown and spotty. Mum hated them once they'd lost their tinge of green. He peeled one and wrapped it in a slice of bread. That was tea sorted, anyway.

He took his phone out of his backpack and put it on to charge, trailing the cable across the kitchen worktop to position the phone on the windowsill. A line of missed calls and a text from Daniel filled the screen. Alex opened the text. Big news? For Daniel that could be anything from getting full marks in his chemistry test to cementing his relationship with Caitlin. Shifting his phone along until he got three bars, Alex called Daniel's mobile. There was no answer.

Face down on cold earth, his cheek bruised from the sharp stones beneath him, Daniel touched the gash in his top lip. His head was throbbing ... yet part of his brain recognised something familiar in his surroundings. On the stone wall beside him he could see ferns growing in a shaft of light that came from an ill-fitting trapdoor above. How he'd got here was beyond him. He closed his eyes and surrendered to the pain at the back of his skull.

SUNDAY

CHAPTER 21

Alex grappled with the sheet, fighting with the wind to get it in the laundry basket, then went along the washing line to get the pillowcases. Black clouds scudded over; swollen drops of rain plopped on his head. So, this was the remains of hurricane Harry the weather forecaster had warned of this morning. 'Travel will be disrupted,' she'd promised in an enthusiastic voice.

Just Mum's duvet cover to gather in, then he could set about sprucing up her bedroom.

He swore as the phone started to ring inside the house. Three, four, five. He counted the telephone trills as he stuffed the duvet cover in the laundry basket and stumbled indoors, willing the phone to keep ringing. Whoever it was, he wouldn't be able to ring back until he'd paid off the rest of the overdue bill.

'Alex Cameron,' he said into the phone.

Two minutes later he almost wished he hadn't got to it in time.

No, Alex had said to Daniel's father, Daniel wasn't round at his. Nor had Alex seen him at the match yesterday.

It was with some embarrassment that he admitted he hadn't seen Daniel since after shinty practice on Thursday.

Alex couldn't even start to imagine where Daniel might be if he wasn't at home or with him at the croft but, remembering Daniel's text, Alex suggested the reverend contact Caitlin. He felt bad not going to the Manse. But it was already well into the afternoon and he had stuff to finish before he could persuade Aunty Joan that the house, at least, was sorted. He didn't want Mum staying at the chalet another night. He wanted her at home, in her own surroundings, eating food that would make her well.

Alex considered taking the Corsa van up to Aunty Joan's. It would take him five minutes by car and at least twenty minutes walking. He'd be able to bring Mum back easily too. He'd learned to drive in a beat-up old car when he'd grown tall enough to see over the steering wheel, with Dad sitting in the passenger seat as they trailed around the fields. But he didn't want Aunty Joan adding underage driving to her complaints.

He went to the barn and put on Dad's old waterproof jacket before setting off. The rain was already getting heavier.

When Aunty Joan answered the door to him at the chalet she was even frostier than yesterday. Alex ducked beneath the small veranda over the door to keep out of the rain. She told him, arms folded across her chest, that Mum had had a good rest and was getting up to have something to eat.

'I've got a mushroom risotto ready,' Alex said. He even had the heel of a Parmesan wedge that Tony had given him with enough cheese left on it to grate over the top.

'She needs food to build her up,' Aunty Joan replied. 'I've made a lamb stew. She's staying with us tonight.'

'I'll just have a chat with her then.' He wasn't going to ask permission to see his own mother. Reluctantly, Aunty Joan stood back to let him in with a 'you'll be lucky,' as an aside.

The stew smelled good and Alex acknowledged he couldn't top that. And he had no means of getting Mum home. No matter what he said he was tied to whatever Aunty Joan decided.

Mum was up and dressed and sitting on a spindly chair with her feet on a pouffe. Alex pulled up a stool from under the kitchen table and sat beside her. She had her hands clasped in her lap and her lips were pinched together, as if she was listening to something she didn't approve of. But she turned to him when he said, 'Mum.'

She didn't answer, although her lips relaxed a little. Not a smile, but a softening at least. The best he could take from that was that she was pleased to see him.

Alex wasn't sure what to do next. Aunty Joan was giving him shifty glances and he, very pointedly, hadn't been asked to stay for tea. And yet it felt wrong to just leave Mum and head back to the croft alone.

The tension in the small kitchen was broken when Stewart came in and threw his car keys on the sideboard. 'Alex. I'm glad you're here,' he said, picking a biscuit out of a jar. 'I just called at the croft ... By the way,' Stewart continued, turning to Mum, 'I found this chap leaning against the door,' and with that he shook the rain off a plastic bag he had in his hand and took out one of Mum's brightly coloured rag dolls. 'Didn't think you'd want him getting drenched,' he said, passing it to her.

Alex was glad of the warmth of voice Stewart used with Mum, but he blanched when he heard the next words Stewart directed at him.

'I've just come to get my waterproofs and a torch. We're meeting at the shop in ten minutes. Constable Logan is organising a team to look for Daniel.'

CHAPTER 22

Alex viewed the chalet through the wing mirror of the Nissan as Stewart fired the engine for the third time to get it started.

Had Alex forgotten something Daniel had told him? Had he been so caught up with Chuck he'd missed something important going on? He could always take a reasonable guess at where Daniel was, at any moment of any day.

Was it their argument—could Daniel have been so pissed off with him that he'd gone off somewhere to lick his wounds. But his last text hadn't suggested that.

Yet Alex was sure of one thing—there was little point going around in circles with what might have happened—a search of the area was definitely what was needed.

Alex thought about the fresh sheets he'd put on Mum's bed and the bunch of flowers waiting for her. He'd scrubbed the kitchen floor and even found a bottle of elderflower cordial at the back of the larder that Mum had made years back. He'd made it up and put a jugful ready in the fridge. This was not how Sunday afternoon should have panned out. Now he had no choice but to leave her at Aunty Joan's again.

In the village centre Stewart pulled up beside five or six other vehicles in the shop car park. Alex could see a huddle of people in the veranda that ran along one side of the shop. In the centre of the huddle was Constable Logan. A couple of police officers with hi-vis jackets were shepherding newcomers. Pulling up their hoods as they both slammed the doors on the Nissan, Alex and Stewart joined the huddle.

Constable Logan had pinned a map to the wooden slats on the back wall of the veranda. She'd drawn a kind of pie-chart with the village at the centre. Two of the five pieces of pie marked out had the coast as their outer boundary. The other three sections trailed off into the hills behind the village. In each section was a scattering of red dots.

When she'd got everybody's attention, Constable Logan explained the plan of action. She wanted people to get into teams with a view to a concentrated search through each section. She suggested each team should choose an area they were most familiar with.

'Each team must have someone with a mobile. Here are the emergency numbers you can call,' she said, giving out slips of paper to those who held up their hands.

Stewart and Alex looked at each other.

'Mine's rather basic,' Stewart said to Constable Logan as she handed him a slip and took note of his mobile number.

Alex jumped when he felt a pinch on his bottom. Turning around, he was pleased to see Moth.

'What's going on?' she asked.

Alex frowned. 'Nobody knows where Daniel is. You haven't seen him, have you?'

Moth's normal cheery expression fell and she shook her head.

'Is your phone charged?' he asked her.

'To the max,' she said.

'Good. Come with us.'

When the teams were sorted out—Alex, Stewart and Moth took the pie slice around Alex's croft—Constable Logan drew attention to the red dots, which were derelict crofts, bothies and such like.

'Make sure you pay particular attention to any places where Daniel might have sought shelter,' she said. 'I've heard from one of Daniel's friends that he's been limping of late. Maybe from a shinty injury. So Daniel may've got into difficulties and needed somewhere to hole up against the weather.'

Caitlin and her dad were in a group that would search one of the upland areas. Their large Alsatian sat obediently beside Caitlin. It must have been her, Alex reckoned, who'd mentioned Daniel's limp to Constable Logan—although he did admit that any one of the shinty players would have said the same if asked.

'Any news ... anything at all ... call in immediately,' Constable Logan went on. 'I'll be here with Reverend Macaulay.'

As the search teams made their ways to their vehicles, Alex saw Reverend Macaulay and Eva sitting in Eva's red Punto—Eva slumped in the driving seat and the reverend in the passenger seat with his elbows on his knees and his head in his hands.

As the sky turned darker and the blackbirds called out their evening songs despite the rain, Alex heard the trill of Stewart's phone. Constable Logan was calling everybody back in. There had been no results from any of the teams but it would be too dark soon for the search to be productive.

Alex, Moth and Stewart had talked endlessly about where Daniel could be while they'd combed their allotted area that extended to the Coffin Road, so named because it was the route over the flank of the hill that had been used in the past by people living in the outlying townships when carrying their coffins to the church. The coffin with Alex's Dad in had left the croft in a hearse and had travelled on the regular road to the church, through the village.

They'd called Daniel's name into the gloom of derelict buildings and little used bothies, shining the torch into copses of close growing trees and dense undergrowth.

But Daniel was still missing.

The three of them trudged the half mile downhill to the croft.

'When did you say you saw him last?' Moth asked as she headed into the barn to return the wellies she'd borrowed. Alex followed her in.

'Will you stop asking me that! I've not seen him since Thursday evening, after shinty practice. Which you know well enough.'

'But he was in school on Friday.'

'I assume so. We were out all day, remember?'

Moth shrugged.

'Are you going home now?' Alex would have liked some company.

'Yeah. Mum's orders.'

'Tell me about it,' Alex said. 'You could help me out though, Moth. You know my mum would be better off back here.'

Moth demurred. 'Not much I can do when Mum has her mind set on something.'

'But you agree with me, don't you? She should be in her own home.'

Moth stood the wellies in line with the other pairs against the barn wall and pulled on her trainers. There was a beep from the Nissan. 'You'll have to leave me out of it. Sorry,' she said, hurrying out.

Alex watched her go. 'Thanks for nothing,' he said to the empty space around him.

Alex was still seething with Moth's lack of faith in him when he waved her and Stewart off to go to their nice lamb stew and a cosy family get-together Sunday evening. And she'd barely disguised her reproach that he didn't know where Daniel had gone. Fucksake. Was he meant to be his minder 24/7? Daniel was only a few days off his seventeenth birthday. He was old enough to look after himself.

Switching on the light in the kitchen, which did nothing to cheer the place at all, Alex took the risotto out of the fridge.

He was so hungry he reckoned he'd manage the whole lot by himself. In fact, how had he ever thought there'd be enough for the two of them? He tipped the solid mass out of the pan into a plastic container and broke it up with a fork. He put it in the microwave, turned the dial to two minutes and pressed the start button. Nothing. No light. No movement of the glass turntable.

He checked the mains socket on the wall thinking he might have unplugged it when he was cleaning the kitchen. It was plugged in and switched on. He turned the dial to one minute and pressed START again. Still nothing. It was fucked. He took out the plastic tub and, leaning against the sink, ate the cold stodgy clumps. The starchy grains clagged against the roof of his mouth.

Moth was right. He was useless.

CHAPTER 23

She meant well. Caitlin knew that. But she couldn't cope with Mum going on so. She'd kept up a barrage of questions since Caitlin and Dad had got back from the search. Was Mum really so blind to the fact that Caitlin could scarcely speak?

'And you say he didn't seem worried about anything?'

'No,' was Caitlin's reply. Again.

'Or over-excited about anything?'

Dad gave a cough as he dished out the stovies Mum had cooked for supper.

Caitlin sat at the table and pushed her fork through the food, trying to block out Mum's ongoing monologue on how Daniel's disappearance seemed so out of character and wondering where he might be.

'And didn't you say it was his birthday—'

'*Is* not *was*. Don't talk about him in the past tense. It *is* his birthday next Monday.' When she started shouting at her mother Caitlin knew it was time to retreat to her room.

Sitting on her bed, she reached into her shoulder bag and took out her wallet. She'd printed out the picture she'd taken of Daniel under the beech tree and trimmed it so that his face and upper body filled the photo window inside her wallet.

Whether Daniel had had some clandestine plan for yesterday that involved him staying away, or whether he'd had an accident and was stuck somewhere, waiting for help to find him, Caitlin didn't know.

And not knowing bothered her.

She peered at his face in the photo, searching his features for a clue. He had a diffidence about him, making him appear uneasy in his surroundings. His brown eyes seemed wary. But the troublesome black hair, which he pushed across his forehead when he wanted to say something important, softened the cornered wild animal look.

Caitlin closed her wallet with the unwelcome thought that yes, if Daniel wanted to keep a secret, then that is exactly what he would do. And come on, she thought, although they had shared a *lot*, they'd only spent a limited amount of time together. That Daniel hadn't told Alex about any possible jaunt—this much had been clear when she'd seen Alex at the search—only confused things further.

She replaced her wallet and lifted the physics revision book off her bedside table. Not that she kidded herself she'd be tackling any of the unfathomable questions, but because it had been Daniel's hands that had delivered it. She blushed at the thought of dashing off to catch a glance of him at shinty practice when he'd already been at her house, dropping off the book to help her catch up.

She'd even forgotten to thank him. Well, there had been more pressing things to do on their first date than talk about physics.

He decided to call it a day with the ongoing cleaning—how had he become accustomed to all this grime? —and was on his way upstairs when the phone started ringing. It was Reverend Macaulay again.

'Alex. I just wanted to thank you for going out to look for Daniel,' he said in a voice that was close to cracking.

'Don't even mention it. I'm sorry there's no news.'

'No ... I'm at a loss to know where he's gone.'

Alex didn't know what to say to that. 'Well ... I'll let you know straight away if I hear anything.'

'I know you will. It's just...' Again, the reverend's voice wavered, 'I just want him back home.' There was another long pause before the reverend went on: 'You see we haven't really spoken about ... important things ... for some time now. My fault I know ... But if he's had any worries ... any concerns ... Well, he won't have told me. That's all.'

'I know what you're saying ... I don't think he was worried ... not especially ... nothing he told me about anyway.'

The reverend cleared his throat before speaking again. 'I did speak to Caitlin, as you suggested. She wasn't aware of anything troubling Daniel either, although I know they've only recently met. She mentioned they'd had a very successful date on Friday and that the only thing bothering

Daniel seemed to be the injury on his leg. He became quite cross about it apparently, especially as they were getting intimate.' The reverend coughed slightly.

Fucksake, did this girl have to share everything? No wonder Daniel wanted a bit of privacy.

'I'm sure he's all right,' Alex said, with what he hoped was a convincing tone.

Alex reckoned there'd be little chance of him getting to sleep. Apart from still feeling restless without Mum in the house, he'd had a thought that he should have checked for Daniel at Chuck's campsite. That section of the coast had been outside the pie-chart search area on the map. It was too dark now to take his boat out. And if Daniel had gone off, wanting some space to himself, he'd be safe enough there.

If only Daniel had left some sort of message.

Alex switched off his bedroom light and got into bed. He only let his head hit his pillow once he'd decided to get up early and go to Chuck's campsite—before he went to see Mum at the chalet—and all that before going to school.

It was a gentle sound that woke him, like a branch tapping on his bedroom window. Alex jumped out of bed before the significance of the rhythm gained a hold in his consciousness. Peering out of the window he could make out the figure of a girl balanced on the stick-shed roof. She had her back to the window but he could see her long hair falling over her shoulders. Yet her stance, as she bent her right knee against the slope of the roof to steady herself was just like ...

Alex lifted the window a fraction and shivered as the damp air hit his bare chest.

The girl turned to him and whispered, 'Let me in then.'

Alex stood back as she clambered over the window frame.

She stood before him, tall and straight, and with her left hand she reached up and pulled her hair away from her head.

There was no way this was true. This could not be real.

Alex felt his legs shake before they folded beneath him. He landed like a sack on the end of his bed.

No wonder the figure had looked familiar. 'Chuck?'

'Hey,' Chuck whispered. 'What's the matter? Aren't you happy to see me?'

'Chuck,' Alex said again. It really was him. With his lithe, athletic body and the supercilious way he held his head.

'I know. I'm an asshole for not letting you know I'd be away for a bit. But you know ... my mum.' Chuck swung the longhaired wig from a finger.

But Chuck was dead. His body washed up, ragged flesh, bloated hands.

'You want to come fishing?' Chuck asked.

Could things get any more unreal?

'Fishing?'

Chuck put his finger to his lips indicating Alex was talking too loudly. 'Yeah. I'm seriously starving.'

'It's the middle of the night.'

'One o'clock actually. I've got a torch.' Chuck stuck his hand in his hoodie pocket and pulled out a slim Maglite. He switched it on and played the pinpoint beam around the bedroom.

Alex wasn't aware of making a conscious decision, yet he pulled on his jeans and jumper. There was no need to follow their established procedure and go out through the bedroom window. There was no Mum to worry about disturbing tonight. But Alex suddenly realised he didn't want Chuck knowing that. So when Chuck donned his wig and turned to exit through the window and skid down the stick-shed roof, Alex followed him.

They kept their voices low as they left the croft, even though Alex knew it was only the beasts around that could hear them.

Chuck could barely suppress his excitement at the prospects of the fishing expedition.

'I'm not taking the boat out,' Alex said when he eventually understood what Chuck was hinting at. 'It's pitch black.'

That wasn't actually true. The moon was over a quarter full and they could see the way well enough. Chuck pointed up to it as if to state the obvious.

'Yeah. But what about those?' Alex said, indicating the bank of clouds out to the east.

'They've already passed over,' Chuck said. 'It's clearing now.'

Alex knew this was also true. He'd been out searching for Daniel when the rain from those very clouds had drenched him.

'Still. It's too ... dark.' He was going to say dangerous but that would only have goaded Chuck into a challenge. Alex had learned well enough that Chuck would never pass on a challenge, no matter what the danger.

'I knew you'd wimp out,' Chuck was saying as he crossed the cattle grid with a few deft strides, balancing neatly on the rails. 'We don't need your precious boat. I brought this.' He rummaged under the hedge and when he stood up again he was holding a fishing rod.

Alex resisted commenting on the wind-up. He was going to be more controlled in his dealings with Chuck. He even held back on the hundreds of questions that were banging in his brain. Chuck wouldn't be able to keep his story to himself for long and Alex wasn't going to give him the satisfaction of being asked.

There was one question that Alex desperately wanted the answer to but even that could keep. Yes. He felt much more in control of things now.

'Daniel enjoying being back at school?' Chuck asked as they tramped along the road, Chuck in the lead.

'He's not around at the moment.' For some reason Alex didn't want Chuck's take on Daniel's disappearance.

'Oh. Shame. I was looking forward to catching up with him.' Chuck turned to look at Alex.

'Yeah. He's gone off on his own for a bit.'

'Getting adventurous, is he?' Chuck went back to staring at the track ahead. 'About time too.'

The moon remained a guiding light and Chuck only used the pencil beam of his Maglite to pick out a few treacherous rock slabs, slick with rainwater, when they reached Alex's cove.

Chuck was responsible for getting a fire going. Alex checked the reel and line on the fishing rod and watched Chuck's nimble fingers, already making quick work of constructing his palm-sized fireball—dripping a few drops of lighter fluid on one of the narrow strips of muslin he kept for this purpose in his camouflage trouser pocket, and interweaving it with the dried moss and grasses he'd gathered. Using his flint lighter, he coaxed a flame in the bundle before placing it within a tiny wigwam of dry twigs on the sand.

With each skilled at their own jobs, they were soon eating char-cooked mackerel and licking oily fingers.

'That seal has been in the same position for ages.' Chuck said. He was stretched out on his stomach, his elbows resting on the sand to stabilise his hold on the binoculars.

The moon's reflection on the water made it easy to see anything that disturbed the glassy surface. Even without the binoculars Alex could see the animal's head poking out before sinking back into the water. 'Probably a good spot for fish.'

'If I was an animal I'd be a seal.' Chuck dropped the binoculars on the sand. He perked up, looking around, impersonating the seal.

Alex laughed, fully agreeing with Chuck's choice. Seals were curious and playful. They were powerful yet graceful in the water and happy enough to lie around basking in the sun. Yes, a good choice, Alex thought.

'What about you? What animal would you be?'

Alex grimaced. He'd never thought about anything like that before. 'Haven't a clue,' he said eventually.

'Come on. Let your imagination go.'

'I can't.' Alex laughed again, more to mask his discomfort this time.

Chuck jumped onto his hands and knees. He let out a roar. 'Grrrrr. How about a lion? Would you be a lion?'

Alex shook his head, confused. Why not a lion? he thought to himself.

'Too aggressive,' he said at last.

'Okay. A barn owl.'

'Have you seen a barn owl hunt a defenceless rodent?'

'I know then,' Chuck said, kneeling up. 'A huge bear!'

Alex frowned.

'A big brown bear, wading through the river to scoop out salmon to feed to its cub waiting on the bank.'

Alex laughed.

'It's true. You'll be a great parent. Caring. Non-judgemental.' Chuck went back beside the fire, his knees tucked under his chin, seemingly uninterested in Alex's response to his suggestion. That he'd made the correct choice was beyond doubt.

Alex considered the image Chuck had conjured up for him. Maybe Chuck had got it right.

Then Chuck shivered, even though he was closest to the fire and he had his hood pulled over his head and the laces tied beneath his chin. 'You got that blue jumper in your boat? The warm one?'

'Blue jumper?' Alex's stomach muscles tightened.

'I borrowed it once. It's in your boat?'

'I thought you still had that,' Alex said, battering down the feeling that a horde of centipedes was squirming up his gullet.

'No. No. I put it back.'

Alex shrugged. 'I'll have a look.' He stood up, knowing full well that Chuck had never returned it. It certainly hadn't been there when he'd got spare clothes for Moth the other day. He wandered over to his boat and made a pretence of rummaging through the locker beneath the seat then pulled out a thin beige sweater with holes in the elbows.

'Here. Stick this on this under your hoodie.' He threw the sweater at Chuck.

'Nice one. Thanks. I'll give it you back tomorrow,' Chuck said, putting the sweater on as Alex suggested.

Then again, could Chuck have put back the navy jumper without Alex knowing ... and someone else had taken it? Somebody who'd gone on to have an accident—got themselves drowned and washed up in his cove? No. It was too unbelievable. But whatever *had* happened, it hadn't been Chuck who'd washed up dead wearing his jumper.

Chuck picked up a stick. 'We're the same, you and me, aren't we, Alex?' He used the stick to scatter the remains of the fire then pitched it into the sea. 'How about, when this is all over, we get some matching tattoos?'

Alex watched Chuck pick up the fishing rod and rest it on his shoulder like a soldier with a rifle on parade.

'What shall we get?' Chuck went on. 'Something classy, like a Celtic knot. One with dragons, their tails intertwining.'

And when Chuck set off on his trek along the shore to his campsite he turned back after a few paces and called, 'You're a real pal, you know.'

The horde of centipedes in Alex's gut found a resting place for a little while as he walked back to the croft. At least Chuck's appearance had saved him a trip to the campsite. Clearly Daniel wasn't there.

MONDAY

CHAPTER 24

He made it to school as the late bell was ringing. The secretary must have seen him hurrying up the road; she was waiting for him at the office hatch with a slip of paper in her hand.

'What is it this time then?' she asked. 'Pine marten in the hen house?'

Alex grunted. 'Overslept.'

The secretary's face turned grim as she pushed the register across the hatch for him to sign. 'Oh, of course, you were out looking for Daniel.'

That answered one of his questions anyway. Alex had been mortified when he slept through his alarm and hadn't been in time on the road as usual. A small part of him had expected, or at least hoped, that Daniel would breeze up to school as if nothing had happened. But Daniel had obviously not made it to school. On time or otherwise.

Alex nodded. He hoped she wouldn't go on; he needed to get to class. But she gave him a concerned smile as she held out the late slip and he was free to go.

Thankfully it was Hospitality first. He stretched his arm along the workbench and rested his head on it while he flipped the pages of recipe books. And Rachael, the girl who'd let him sit beside her without complaining too much, was even prepared to make comments on his suggestions for a meal plan. Their assignment 'showstopper' three course meal had to be nutritionally balanced as well as stunningly presented. With the choice of menu titles, *A Highland Larder* or *Autumn on the Shore*, Alex was soon considering possible ingredients.

Rachael poked him in the arm. 'Have you finished your costings?' she whispered.

Alex shook his head. He'd scribbled some recipe ideas in his jotter, planning to bring in as many ingredients as possible from the croft. The school stocked basics, but for a showstopper he'd be responsible for supplying the main ingredients from his own pocket. And there was no money in any of his pockets.

Caitlin left the biology lab early before midmorning break and waited for Alex outside the English classroom. Unsurprisingly, he was first out. Alex wasn't the type to stay behind and ask questions, currying favour with the teacher.

It wasn't only his muscular bulk that set him apart from the other boys in his year, she thought as Alex bowled past her, but his gruff expression and his rounded shoulders. He wore his displeasure with the world like a force field.

'You going out?' Caitlin asked as she followed in his slipstream, almost stumbling over her own feet.

'What's it to you?'

'Can I walk with you?'

'What on earth would possess me to want to walk with you?'

She wasn't going to be put off by open hostility. 'You know something. Something you're not telling me.'

'Round of applause for Miss Marple.'

Caitlin grabbed Alex's shirt sleeve as he tried to pitch himself against a tide of S4 girls rushing up the stairs. 'His leg. There was something going on, I know it.'

Pleased that Alex's second attempt to get downstairs was foiled by raucous S4 boys following behind the S4 girls, she dropped the level of her voice and said, 'Was it some of the lowlife? Have they been bullying Daniel? He was cross about whatever—'

'Oh. He was *cross*, was he?'

Nor was she going to be put off by a pathetic attempt at sarcasm. She kept a tight hold on Alex's sleeve. 'Yes. He was. He was *cross, annoyed,* whatever word you wish to use.'

'But he chose not to tell you about it.'

Caitlin clenched her teeth.

'I can assure you,' Alex went on, 'I'm certain that Daniel's injury has nothing whatsoever to do with him not being here.'

'Not being here ... You make it sound like he's popped down the shops. He's disappeared for God's sake!'

'Well, he's nearly seventeen. He's allowed some space if he needs it ... From both of us,' Alex said with a finality even Caitlin couldn't ignore.

She let go of his sleeve and watched Alex hurry down the now empty stairs.

'You can't be certain,' she yelled down the stairwell.

The group of S2 kids who'd been watching her ran off giggling when she turned her glare on them.

Outside, Caitlin leaned against the fence. The babble from the kids indoors was driving her crazy. She needed a quiet space to check her mobile.

Nothing. Why would there be an answer to her latest message when he hadn't answered any of the others she'd sent? The anxiety caused by Daniel's disappearance was being compounded by her not knowing whether Daniel couldn't or wouldn't reply.

She screwed up her eyes when she sensed imminent tears. She wasn't going to let her emotions interfere with her actions.

Her mobile buzzing in her hand shook her out of her self-absorption. It was a text from Constable Logan wanting to know if Caitlin knew Daniel's computer or email password. She texted back immediately her two-word answer: Sorry. No.

But that didn't mean she wouldn't try to find out.

Back in the lab she logged in to the school network. There might be a chance that Daniel used the same password for school and home.

A bunch of pupils were waiting to get into the Craft portacabin after lunch. With so much to sort out at home, Alex would have preferred to be at the croft instead of joining them. But only this morning he'd promised mum he would be in school. 'And make sure you turn up to all your classes,' Aunty Joan had added.

Their teacher, Mr Brownlow, was making his way from the main building but came to a halt as Angus, a boy in S6, rushed out behind him and handed over a sheet of paper.

'Seems young MacKay here hasn't the brains for geography so he'll be joining our merry band of ne'er-do-wells from today,' Mr Brownlow said as he reached the group. The class was used to his quips about how his subject was perceived by the guidance teachers as an easier option.

'Ahem.' A false cough came from the bunch of pupils waiting by the door.

'Aye, aye. All except you, Davis,' the teacher continued as he pushed his way through them to unlock the workshop door. Fiona Davis was determined to get into dentistry and had passed a whole raft of Highers with requisite grades last year. She was taking Craft to demonstrate her outstanding manual dexterity when she went to interviews.

'Now if you don't mind ... as we're already late...' Mr Brownlow held the door open as they all shuffled in. 'And remember, task one, with associated paper work, to be on my desk by the end of tomorrow.'

That being the only instruction necessary, the class got busy.

Alex was rubbing down the base of his table lamp, and was so absorbed in his sanding, it was only when the teacher shouted, 'Alex Cameron, are you deaf?' that he realised he was being called over.

'You're furthest on,' the teacher said pointing at Alex. 'Go over the learning intentions and the assessment criteria with MacKay here. And show him where to find the tasks online. Oh ... after that show him your project.'

Great. He really should have gone home. Angus was so full of himself, thinking himself so cool riding his classic Lambretta to school. Even though they rarely crossed paths, Alex felt uneasy around him. Who was he kidding? Other than Daniel, Alex never felt comfortable with any of the lads in school.

Waving a hand to dismiss them, Mr Brownlow turned to the queue that had built up on the other side of his desk where students clutched half-worked projects or broken woodworking tools.

'You should ask for a cut of his wages,' Angus said as he followed Alex to the computer base in an annex next to the workshop.

CHAPTER 25

Alex slammed the door of the chalet as he left, knowing it would only make matters worse, but unable to control his feelings.

He'd been shocked when he'd got to Aunty Joan's after school. Mum was sitting on the same spindly chair but she was completely closed off in her own world, barely acknowledging him when he spoke to her. And, even scarier, she was clutching the rag doll Stewart had brought up yesterday as if she depended on it for her life.

Aunty Joan was still going on about the phone at the croft being 'unavailable' as she politely put it. She'd looked moderately impressed when Alex had insisted the bill was his responsibility and he would deal with it, but she went on to say it was *reasonable* to get that sorted before Mum went home.

Alex hated leaving Mum like that but Aunty Joan had made it quite clear there was no other option.

He was still battling against her arguments in his head when he got home, so he almost missed it as he stormed in the back door. It was propped in a corner of the square lobby, next to the door to Mum's workroom, its pink floral dress and rosy cheeks looking cheery in the beam of sunlight that sloped in through the small high window. Alex lifted the rag doll and examined it. This was the third—or was it the forth counting the one Stewart had picked up?

Alex hadn't given much thought to the others. He hadn't got headspace to think about anything that wasn't pressing for immediate attention. If quizzed about it, he'd have said that maybe a fox had somehow found its way into a box of dolls and was littering them around the place. But this one? Well, for one thing, it was *inside* the house. No way could a fox open the door, drop the rag doll and close the door again.

Then again—maybe the dolls *had* been scattered beyond the croft by an animal and a neighbour was finding them and dropping them off? Whatever was going on, he decided he would lock the doors before leaving for school in the morning.

But right now, his most pressing problem was sorting out the phone bill.

He got nowhere with the phone line providers, using his mobile to call them, standing outside the kitchen window for the best signal. It was a lengthy procedure to get the numbers checked for errors, the customer service person had said, obviously not believing he hadn't made the calls either. Could he not borrow the money in the meantime? was her only suggestion.

He hated the thought of it, but there was no other way. He needed the quickest means of earning the most cash.

Up in his bedroom he unlocked his desk drawer and took out the list of websites Chuck had given him. At the bottom were a couple of sites Chuck had put stars next to, telling Alex at the same time that the punters on those would pay more—but it wouldn't be just his upper torso he would need to prepare. Alex had sworn he would never stoop to using them.

He fitted the webcam to his computer. Then, repulsed by its synthetic feel, he seized hold of the black curly wig and headed to the bathroom.

TUESDAY

CHAPTER 26

With only a few minutes to the lunchtime bell Alex was rushing to finish the CAD rendering exercise on a cuboid image Mr Brownlow had set the class. He was actually grateful that the task had distracted him enough to stop him thinking about Daniel for a little while. Two nights. Where had he gone? Where was he sleeping? Why hadn't he at least sent a message? Surely the police knew how to trace people who went missing?

Alex cast an eye around the computer base. Most of the others were already logging off, pushing away their chairs, chatting and joking amongst themselves, but a few were still at their workstations. Alex could see Angus' legs ending in his red Skechers under the bench a few spaces along from him. Angus was focused on his computer screen. At least he was attempting to catch up, but Alex wasn't going to keep helping him out as he had again today— getting behind with his own tasks as a result.

The CAD programme completed the final rendering operation and Alex saved and closed his file. But as he pushed back his chair and was about to take out his earphones he heard a bing. An envelope symbol on his task bar showed a message had come to his school email account.

The message, when he opened it, contained just one word: Interesting? There was a paperclip attachment symbol and Alex clicked on that too. A thumbnail image opened in the top left corner of his monitor. It took less than a fraction of a second for Alex to realise what the picture was and he hurriedly closed the image.

It wasn't a full frontal. More of a sideways view. The glistening flesh on display was from his shoulder to his buttock, the only so-called garment to be seen was a black leather shoelace tied tightly around his left bicep. His face was in profile, his angular cheek bones softened by the black curly wig.

Alex swivelled around in his seat, checking to see if anyone had been looking his way. Seemed not. Everybody was still going about their own business.

Who'd sent it? Going back to his mail account Alex saw the sender ID was AM6. He reckoned there must be a few kids in school with the initials AM but there was only one in S6. Angus MacKay.

Turning away from his work station, Alex could see Angus had already packed up and was heading out of the door in the knot of the S6 pupils claiming their privilege of leaving before the bell.

Alex grabbed his backpack and pushed his way to the front of the queue waiting for Mr Brownlow's say-so to leave. No way was Angus getting to walk away from this.

Racing to catch up with them, Alex saw the group cross the car park before three of them peeled off towards the S6 common room, leaving Angus on his own to enter the main building.

Alex's breathing quickened as his rage intensified. He followed Angus through the front doors—into the empty foyer. He called his name. And as Angus turned, Alex shot a fist towards his face.

* * *

Dinner duty. Caitlin hated it. Marshalling a queue of fidgety kids waiting to get their lunch. But with the hope of getting a good reference, it was just another thing to put up with. And it was only once a week. The queue was mostly younger kids, the seniors usually finding items of dubious nourishment in the local shop to get them through the afternoon.

She was trying to sort out a group of lads gambling with coins against a wall when a clutch of S1 girls came rushing towards her. 'Miss. Come quick.'

'Don't call me Miss.' What was it with these new first years? Couldn't they tell from her uniform that she was a pupil the same as them?

'Some lads are fighting, Miss,' a tall girl said, pointing towards the front door.

This isn't happening, Caitlin thought as she followed the girls and saw Alex and Angus grabbing at each other's clothes and swinging fists.

Sitting outside the depute's office before afternoon classes started was as shameful as it had always been. The office door swung open and Angus exited, strutting down the corridor without a backward glance.

'Okay, Alex. You next,' the depute said in the whiney voice Alex hated so much.

'...appropriate behaviour ... example to the younger pupils.' Alex had heard it all before. Not for a while, though. He'd managed to keep below the radar for some time now.

The whiney voice stopped. Alex had caught an inflection at the end of the sentence. He'd been asked a question.

'Sorry, Sir?' Alex said.

'I was saying ... I know you can look after yourself, but I do need to know if any bullying is going on.'

'Thought you told us there is no bullying at this school, Sir.'

'And so there isn't. Unless you wish to inform me otherwise.'

Alex shook his head then glanced at the clock on the wall. 'If you don't mind, I'll be late for English.'

The depute stood up. 'Well, we can't have you leaving my office thinking fighting is an appropriate way to settle your petty disputes. I'll see you for detention...'

Not after school. Not with everything at home to sort out to Aunty Joan's satisfaction before she'd allow Mum back.

'...Tomorrow lunchtime,' the depute said moving towards the door, conversation over.

Which left Alex wondering as he charged up the stairs to the English classroom, just how had Angus got that picture?

He wasn't going to let this become a routine. Get out of school as quick as possible, try to avoid arguing with Aunty Joan while visiting Mum, then tramp back to the lonely croft.

He wasn't going to get trapped in a regime where other people's ideas became the reality. He would never get Mum home if Aunty Joan had anything to do with it.

How had he got into this mess in the first place? Fucksake, even Daniel had gone so far as to think he needed some sort of protection.

By the time Alex put the key in his back door his brain was aching with going over and over what needed sorting.

Getting Mum back home had to be top of the list.

He took the laundry basket upstairs and gathered together clothes from his bedroom floor.

Yet finding out where Daniel had gone was equally important. They'd been almost inseparable for forever. How had he not known what had been going on in Daniel's head?

'Think. Think,' he said, whacking his forehead with his fist on each word.

Chuck's pound coin was on his bedside table. He picked it up, flicked it in the air and before he'd caught it on its descent remembered the time Chuck had used the coin to select a cliff to jump off into the sea. Daniel had chickened out that time.

Christ. Daniel had always been scared to death of the sea and Alex had only just got him up to his chest in a gently-swelling tide earlier in the summer. It didn't bear thinking about—but what if Daniel had gone off to try on his own?

'This is even crazier than I thought,' Moth said, sitting upright in the boat as Alex rowed around the headland and followed the coast of the peninsula.

The small boat pitched about in the currents and although Alex was a strong oarsman, navigating a way around the jagged rocks that skirted the coastline was challenging even for him. But the cliff was miles to reach by land, over rough and boggy terrain. Getting there by sea was quicker.

'You sure we need to check for him out here?' Moth continued.

Alex owed her some sort of explanation. She'd come out with him without any question. 'I'm a bit worried he might have done something stupid.'

Moth's face looked like she was holding something back. Alex realised what he'd said. 'Not like that,' he said quickly. 'Nothing *intentional*.'

'What *do* you mean then?'

Alex hesitated. 'We did a few dares.' He didn't need to mention Chuck. 'I just want to check he hasn't taken in into his thick head to try something on his own.'

'You reckon he'd do that?'

Alex shrugged. 'Who the fuck knows what he'd do? Not me apparently.'

It was futile. Their search was a complete waste of time. The only consolation was—as Moth pointed out—finding nothing was better than finding, well, anything.

Daniel knew where he was. He paced the five steps from the stone wall behind him to the stone wall ahead of him, turned and paced the five steps back again. Then turning to a corner of his underground cell he unzipped his jeans, arched his back and let out a stream of stinging piss before carefully tucking himself back.

He'd been here with Alex, when they were kids and had liked frightening themselves stupid. They would lift the trapdoor, which was sunk into one of the gravel paths around the gardens, peer into the dungeon, and make up stories about the ghosts of people who'd been trapped and died there. Another time they'd brought a knotted rope with them. They'd tugged the trapdoor to one side and fixed the rope to the metal ring in its centre. Taking turns, one of them scaled down the sides of what they'd found out was the old ice cellar, holding on to the rope while the other stayed safe in the daylight above. Once Alex had asked Daniel to put the trapdoor back over while he was still down there. Daniel hadn't wanted to do it. 'What for?' Daniel had asked.

Alex had said he didn't know. 'Just do it,' he'd said. And Daniel had. He'd slid the trapdoor back into its countersunk gutter and counted to the prearranged one hundred. Alex hadn't said anything when he climbed back out, holding on to the rope with white knuckles.

Daniel sidled away from the corner to place himself dead centre of what he reckoned was the most northerly wall. The fissures between the stone blocks looked marginally deeper on this side. Finding the tiny holds with his fingertips, and then with the toes of his trainers, he climbed about half the way up before his arms gave way and he fell back heavily to the ground.

He screamed as his sore leg twisted beneath him on landing and he panted through the pain that only gradually let go its tight grip.

Pulling himself into a sitting position he leaned against the wall. He'd known all along, anyway, that the trapdoor was in the centre of the ceiling and wasn't going to be reached by climbing the walls.

WEDNESDAY

CHAPTER 27

Alex sat out the lunch break upstairs in the library, watching through a window that overlooked the front of the building, waiting for Angus to come back from the shop. He was easy to spot as he rounded the bend from the village and approached the school with his bunch of S6 cronies. Alex saw a couple of them charge up the road to plague a lad who was walking on his own.

Alex dashed down the library stairs and positioned himself just inside the front door. When Angus eventually sidled through it he said, 'Angus. A word.'

'Aye, aye. All right?' Angus said, following Alex to the space beneath the stairs where they couldn't be seen.

'So?' Angus said with his back to the wall.

'That picture,' Alex started, beginning to lose his nerve. 'You're not going to...? You never told me how you got it.'

'Like I had a chance.'

'Yeah. Right. I'm sorry.'

'Accepted. No harm done,' Angus said placing his hand on his face where Alex's fist had failed to make contact.

One little gesture to let Alex know he was a rubbish fighter. But Alex continued, 'So?'

'Hmm. Funny thing really. Is there somebody who doesn't like you very much?'

Alex shrugged. 'What do you mean?'

'Sent to my school email account. Anonymously. Well, not from any of my contacts.' Angus gave him a shifty smile. 'Fair put the willies up you yesterday, if you don't mind me saying.'

Alex couldn't understand it. He was convinced Angus must have recognised him during some sordid internet trawling.

Angus took a step towards Alex so that his lips were almost touching Alex's ear. 'No need to worry though. I know how to be discreet. Your secret's safe.' He tapped a finger against the side of his nose in a melodramatic gesture. Except as he lowered his hand his knuckles brushed against Alex's crotch.

It could have been an accident due to their close proximity, but the way Angus, almost imperceptibly, raised his eyebrows, Alex wasn't so sure.

Caitlin saw the police van in the drive when she got home and her heart began to race. This was it. She stood for a moment in the porch to quash the words reverberating in her head, *we've found his body, we've found his body,* before pushing open the front door.

They were in the kitchen. She could hear their muted voices. It sounded like both Mum and Dad were there with Constable Logan.

'Caitlin?' Mum called. 'We're in here.'

They were sitting around the kitchen table. Drinking tea?

Dad stood up when he saw her. 'Come on in, love. Constable Logan has been waiting for you to get back from school,' he said as Caitlin squeezed past the back of Mum's chair.

'You've found him?' Caitlin blurted out.

Constable Logan turned in her seat to face Caitlin, 'I'm sorry. No. We do have some news to share about Daniel. But so far nothing definite to say where he is.'

'Some news?'

Constable Logan went on: 'A couple from the village, and the bus driver, remember seeing Daniel on the early bus on Saturday morning.' She gave Caitlin a questioning stare. 'You wouldn't happen to know where he was going?'

Caitlin shook her head. 'No ... No idea.'

'We've got CCTV footage of Daniel getting off the bus, but nothing after that I'm afraid.'

Dad sat down again and pushed a mug of tea towards Caitlin. It was like an alien object to her.

'We're doing all we can to find Daniel. But if there is anything, any little thing, that you think might help us ... Well, you know how to get hold of me.'

Caitlin nodded. She could feel the tears behind her eyes. 'I don't know anything,' she said.

The expression on Constable Logan's face softened a little. She lifted a manila folder from the table. 'Caitlin. I know you're upset about Daniel and, as I said, we're doing everything we can to—'

'Sitting here isn't d—' Caitlin's mum gave her a look. Constable Logan didn't miss a beat, '... to find him. But I was hoping I could ask you to help me with something else.' She opened the folder and took out two photographs. 'I've shown these to your parents but I'd like you to have look too.'

She placed the photographs on the table, side by side. Both were of items of clothing. The one on the left was a pair of boyfriend-cut blue jeans and a pair of well-worn trainers. The photograph on the right was a navy-blue crewneck jumper. There was a white emblem on the cuff of one sleeve that looked like an anchor. Caitlin didn't recognise it as any particular brand. Maybe it was some yachty designer label.

'You don't know who might own these clothes do you?' Constable Logan was asking as Caitlin examined the pictures on the table.

'No. Is it important?'

'I'm doing a house-to-house enquiry. These are the clothes the girl was wearing. The girl found on the beach.'

'The girl on the beach?'

'I'm sorry,' Constable Logan said, 'I don't want to distress you any further. But if you did recognise the clothes...'

Comprehension dawned on Caitlin. 'The body of the girl?'

'It's all right, Caitlin,' Dad said. 'You've had a good look. If you don't know ... well, you don't know. That's all there is to say.'

'Psst,' Alex heard as he climbed the hill to the chalet, his head bent down.

Moth was lurking amongst the dense rhododendrons that lined the track up to the maze of chalets.

'What's going on?'

'I've sneaked out. Mum would go apeshit if she knew I'd told you.'

'Told me what?'

Moth beckoned him towards where she was hidden in the bush.

'Fucksake, Moth. What is it?'

'I've taken a big risk coming out. You could at least be polite.'

A risk? Of being told off by Aunty Joan? Moth's level of risk-taking needed serious evaluating.

'The police were up before. With photos of the clothes that girl was wearing.'

Moth paused, presumably for Alex to show his appreciation of her as an informer.

'And?' Alex said.

'She—the girl—was wearing a navy jumper. And Mum recognised it as the one she knitted for you.'

Alex hesitated for a moment. 'How could that happen?'

'Yeah, well. Mum said maybe you'd given it to the Oxfam shop because she'd never seen you wearing it, and maybe the girl got it like that.'

'That sounds possible.'

'Only possible if you did give it to the Oxfam shop.'

'I suppose so,' Alex said.

'So did you?'

Alex didn't want to lie but he couldn't come up with an alternative. 'Maybe my mum did,' he said.

Moth eyed him. 'Well ... *my* mum's on the warpath. I thought I'd warn you.'

Alex knew she deserved some thanks. 'Cheers, Moth. I owe you.'

Moth shrugged. 'Give it five minutes,' she said before heading up the hill.

Mum looked tired when Alex stepped into the chalet a few minutes later. And from the look of her tousled hair she'd obviously not been long out of bed.

Moth was putting two pieces of white sliced in the toaster. 'You want a bit?' she asked Alex, holding up another piece.

'Er. Yeah, thanks.'

'Mum's busy in the salon. I'm in charge of making tea. We're having beans on toast,' Moth was saying as Alex pulled up his usual stool beside Mum.

Alex wanted to take hold of her hand but she had them clasped in her lap.

'You should see the size of your pumpkin now,' he said and Mum turned to look at him properly. He'd joked with her earlier in the spring about her wanting to grow a pumpkin in the polytunnel, especially as neither of them really liked the stringy flesh that much.

Mum gave him a questioning look and, smiling, lifted her hands as if cradling a ball.

'Nah. Much bigger,' Alex said.

He was grateful of the space to chat to Mum with only Moth in the kitchen, concentrating on her chores. He was dying to tell her he'd almost paid the phone bill and that the reconnection would be soon but was too scared. What if she asked where he was getting the money?

The mood in the room changed immediately when Aunty Joan came in wearing her hairdresser's overall, a comb and scissors poking out from a front pouch pocket.

'I'll be another half an hour,' she said to Moth. Then seeing Alex, she added her usual welcome. 'How was school then?'

'Fine thanks, Aunty Joan.' He wasn't going to get riled by her today. He would hold it together until he got Mum home. 'I was just telling Mum how well the hens are laying at the moment. And we have a ton of tomatoes to get through.'

'Hmm,' Aunty Joan said before swinging back to her salon in the shed.

It was after he'd left the chalet and was heading down the hill that Alex heard his name being called. Aunty Joan was standing at the doorway of the shed. He really wanted to ignore her but he turned back and joined her.

'I know you've been up to something. I can read the signs.'

Alex studiously avoided her glare.

'So don't you go thinking I'm letting our Cath back with you until I know what it is.'

'You can't...' Alex began, but held back the rest of his words.

'Aye, butter wouldn't melt, would it?'

Alex allowed himself a glance at her acid expression.

'Unless there's anything you want to tell me the now...'

Alex shrugged. 'I don't know what you're on about.'

'Right then. But as I say—I'll get to the bottom of it.'

He was sitting at the kitchen table, calculating the remaining balance of the phone bill, when he heard the back door open and close. Stunned, he watched Angus step into the kitchen.

'Didn't think you were the type to lock your door.'

Alex considered the comment. Angus must have been here before him and tried the door.

Angus nodded towards the sheet of paper on the table and, with a grin that was close to a smirk, said, 'Getting your homework done?'

Alex folded the paper and slid it into his jeans pocket. He glanced at the kitchen door.

'Don't worry. I'm on my own.'

Alex stood up and moved away from the table, maintaining his eye contact with Angus. 'What is it? What do you want?'

'I reckon we've a bit of unfinished business,' Angus said, straightening his shoulders.

Alex's hands clenched into fists at his sides. 'What do you mean?'

Angus stepped up close.

With sweat pricking the back of his neck Alex took a deep breath. He saw Angus reach out a hand. Then felt

Angus' fingers stroke the side of his face and gently pinch his earlobe.

What the fuck was going on?

Angus lowered his hand and Alex felt it skim his shoulder and the length of his arm, lingering for a moment on his clenched hand.

Shit. Alex took in Angus' crisply ironed shirt and the smell of a citrusy aftershave. Could it be possible that Angus wasn't here as a wind up? Or to blackmail him?

Could this be for real?

'When you're ready ... you know where I am,' Angus said before sliding out of the croft as smoothly as he'd entered.

Alex slumped back on the chair and put the back of his hand against his face to cool his flushed cheek.

CHAPTER 28

In the quiet of the kitchen, he'd barely counted a dozen of his banging heartbeats when he heard the rattle of a vehicle over the cattle grid. Not just any vehicle either. He thought he recognised the low rumble made by the police van. A quick glance out of the kitchen window confirmed it. At least with Moth's heads-up he was better prepared for the visit.

When Alex answered Constable Logan's knock on the back door he let his bulk block the doorway. He wouldn't ask her in.

'I'm sorry your Mum's not so well.'

Alex was forced into being polite by her voiced concern. 'She'll be better soon.'

'I'm sure. The doctor will give her something to get her on her feet in no time, heh?'

'Doctor?'

'Sorry. Didn't mean to be nosy. It's just that your aunt mentioned the doctor was with her when I called there this afternoon.'

'Oh, yeah. Right.'

The doctor had been to see Mum and this was the first he was hearing about it?

Constable Logan looked down at her feet then back at Alex. 'Alex, I need to ask you a few questions. And ask a favour of you. Can we go inside?'

Again, politeness won. 'Yeah, all right.'

'Wow. You've been busy. Your Mum will be proud of you,' Constable Logan said as they passed into the kitchen.

Did she really think she could get around him with a lame compliment? And a backhanded one at that. All right. So, the mugs were clean, the top of the stove didn't have a selection of spills from last week's dinners over it and the pans were on their shelf. But when she'd been before she must have clocked all the mess.

He didn't ask her to sit down and they both stood, either side of the square kitchen table. Constable Logan took a plastic document wallet out of a briefcase she was carrying.

'You'll have seen these,' she said, holding up the document wallet to show a Missing Person poster with a photograph of Daniel. 'I've put some around the village and some in town, obviously. I wonder if you could take a few and put them any place I've missed.'

Alex nodded. 'Of course.'

'The more places the better. And don't worry about folk not knowing Daniel where you put them. We're widening our search now.'

Alex hated hearing about the search. 'Anything I can do, just let me know,' he said as Constable Logan put a pile of posters on the table.

'Thanks. There is one other thing. We've got Daniel's laptop. The team have managed a quick look through it—nothing obviously amiss as far as we could see—but we couldn't get into his email account. He must be good at making up passwords. I was wondering if you know it?'

Alex shook his head. 'He's very particular about that. Won't even let on his password at school.'

'I suspected as much. I'll keep the team on it for now.'

Constable Logan's stance suggested she hadn't finished. Alex braced himself for the inevitable.

'You'll probably know I'm investigating the circumstances surrounding the young lass found on the shore.'

Alex shrugged.

'I've some photos of the clothes she was wearing at the time. Could you have a quick look? See if they jog any memories.'

Alex couldn't stop an image coming into his head of the body as it would be now. Probably laid out on a mortuary table, with just a sheet to hide her gender. And her face. Completely gone. A wave of nausea threatened to submerge him.

He pulled a chair from under the table and sat down. Constable Logan did the same. She placed the two pictures on the table and Alex peered at them.

'I've got a jumper like that,' he said, pointing to it in the photograph.

'Have you now?' Constable Logan's tone was only mildly questioning. Nothing too heavy. 'And have you still got it, Alex? Is it here?'

Alex screwed up his nose. 'Nah. It's not really my style. I keep it in the boat in case I get cold when I'm out fishing.'

'So it's in your boat then?' Her tone was a little more pressing now.

'Actually, I know it isn't,' Alex answered. 'I looked out some clothes for Moth the other day and it wasn't there.'

'You think somebody might have taken it?'

'No idea. I didn't really bother too much.'

'If we knew it *was* your jumper the girl was wearing, that would be a big help to us. It would tell us she'd been in this area before she—'

'There's probably loads of jumpers like it, though. Aunty Joan knit it for me. She gets these magazines. I bet lots of aunties and grannies knit exactly the same one for Christmas presents.'

'You could be right.'

Why hadn't he thought of that before? He *could* be right.

'But if you wouldn't mind taking a look at it. I've got it at the station,' Constable Logan persisted.

'Sure.'

'That's great. I knew you would want to help. And while we're there, maybe you could provide a DNA sample so that we can eliminate any traces of yours that we find. If it is your jumper, of course.'

What the...?

'Why do you need ...' Alex started. But it would look odd to refuse. And so what? All it would prove was if it was his jumper. 'All right,' he said.

'That's great. And don't worry. A lot of people are a bit taken aback when we ask for a DNA sample. You can come with me now if that's convenient. It won't take a moment and I can give you a lift back.'

'Go with you?'

'We just use a swab, a bit like a cotton bud, to take a few cells from the inside of your cheek. It's better done at the station,' she said, getting up.

Alex had no option but to follow her.

A rectangular tin and a small packet hit the ground. As he looked up to the open trapdoor, his eyes almost closing against the sudden bright light, he yelled up, 'What do you know about Ellie?'

A bottle of water just missed his head before landing on the ground.

'Tell me,' he yelled at the trap door as it was lowered into place.

Daniel picked up the tin—sardines in tomato sauce. His guts cramped with just the thought of food. It had a type of opening he hadn't seen before. A long key was glued to the base of the tin. He released it and found a tab on the lid that fitted into the slot of the key. With a few turns of the key he exposed the silvery fish in their bed of red gunk. He placed the open tin on large stone and picked up the packet. Cheesy biscuits. Salty—meaning he'd need to drink more water. He would ration this bottle, only taking sips when he was really desperate. He threw the packet aside and set about the sardines, using his grimy fingers to pick out the chunks.

He'd stopped trying to understand why he was here. His capture had obviously been intended. No case of mistaken identity. He'd ruled out being taken as a hostage first off. His father wasn't rich. But he couldn't deny he must be part of some sort of plan. He was being kept alive for some reason.

Caitlin's worst fear was if Mum and Dad found out she'd missed school. Corrine would see her get off the school bus and, although they rarely entered school together, there was still a chance that Corrine would notice her not going in. She sorted that problem when everybody had gone to bed, sneaking into Corrine's bedroom after giving a gentle tap on the door.

Corrine was a hump under her duvet but Caitlin saw she was still wearing her headphones. Caitlin sat on the edge of the bed and Corrine slipped one earpiece to the back of her head.

'I need to go to town tomorrow. Personal stuff,' Caitlin whispered.

'So?'

'I don't want Mum and Dad to know.'

Corrine didn't look too worried about the news.

'But I want somebody to know where I am.'

'No problem,' Corrine said.

Had that gone too easily? But it was only a trip to town. No big deal.

'Will you drop a note in the office for me?'

Corrine looked suspicious now. 'A fake note?'

'Well, it will have to be. In case they check on my whereabouts.

Corrine considered while reaching a hand around to replace her earpiece. 'Okay.'

THURSDAY

CHAPTER 29

She waited for the majority of the other passengers to get off before pulling up her hood and edging out of her seat. She trundled down the centre aisle of the bus and jumped on to the pavement without making eye contact with the driver.

A row of benches ran parallel to the bus stances. Caitlin sat beside a woman with a tartan shopping trolley. Was there any point in doing this? It had seemed a good idea last night. At least she'd be doing something. She wanted to experience it for herself, wanted to go through the same journey as Daniel. The last journey anybody knew he'd made.

Glancing around, Caitlin identified the CCTV camera that had picked up Daniel getting off the bus and turning towards town. It was fixed in one position, aimed at the bus stances.

What was it Daniel needed to do that he couldn't tell anybody about?

Caitlin became aware that the woman beside her had spoken.

'Sorry,' Caitlin said.

'You going to Glasgow?' the woman repeated.

'Er, no.'

'I need a new vest,' the woman clattered on. 'You can only get the ones I like in Dunnes.'

'Oh, right.' Caitlin wasn't paying proper attention to why the woman needed to go to Glasgow, but her question had shaken up Caitlin's thoughts. What if Daniel had planned to head on somewhere else?

There was a noticeboard on the wall with all the bus timetables on. Caitlin got up to look at it. If he was waiting for a connection it must have been for a bus that left after the village bus got in. And on a Saturday. She traced her finger down the list of buses departing on a Saturday. There were services to Glasgow, Perth and Stirling, all leaving within forty to fifty minutes after the village bus got in. He could have been planning to catch any one of those. But, she calculated, scanning all the timetables, if he was coming back the same day there wouldn't be time for him to get to Glasgow before he'd need to get one back to connect with the last bus home. There was a return bus from Perth that just got in in time though.

Whatever his plans—if he had intended to travel further—he hadn't got on another bus. The CCTV camera would have picked him up if he had.

Unless he had been getting a train.

She kicked her foot against the wall. This was getting her nowhere. Maybe she needed to come back on Saturday—if Daniel hadn't turned up by then. She could bring one of the Missing Person posters with her and ask people around the bus and train stations if anybody had seen him.

No. That wouldn't do. A proper reconstruction would be better. The police needed to get this organised. She'd go see Constable Logan as soon as she got back to the village.

'Bye then, hen,' the woman with the tartan shopping trolley said as Caitlin, preoccupied, strode past her.

* * *

Alex scanned the bowed heads of the thirty odd pupils bent over desks, labouring away on their PHSE worksheet in the almost silent room. He'd completed the first page on fire extinguishers, getting the answers, as they'd been told to, from the *Accidents in the Home* booklet they'd each been given. Which extinguishers to use on different types of fire probably was relevant to know but surely they could just be allowed to read the booklet?

He turned over the worksheet. At the top of the next page there was a cartoon of a woman in high heels standing on a stool in a kitchen reaching for something on top of a cupboard. She was balancing on one leg, on tiptoe, to stretch that few extra centimetres higher.

It was more than Alex could endure. He took up his pencil and scored through the page with four or five angry strokes, breaking the pencil in two before placing it on the desk. He stood up, banging his knees on the desk and knocking over his chair, which thudded to the floor.

The Gaelic teacher roped in to teach this shit lifted his gaze from his book and briefly made eye contact but Alex was on his way out of the door.

A few determined strides got him to the portacabin door. Resting his hand on the handle he looked out through the window. A light shower of rain was coming straight down. Sunlight caught the drops as they fell. A solitary herring gull was stamping on the grass, doing its impersonation of Riverdance, before driving its beak in to the turf, searching for the unearthed worms. But Alex couldn't push the door handle down. His promise to his mum was like razor wire trapping him in.

'Hey. Alex.'

Alex spun on his heels. Angus had crept up beside him.

Alex stared into his blue eyes. *If he even dares to touch me ... even with one little finger ...* Alex's hands clenched.

'You coming back or what?' Angus said before turning away and walking towards the classroom.

CHAPTER 30

Thankfully they were in the workshop for their afternoon tech class and Alex could lose himself buffing up the wax finish on his table lamp base. The final stage was to fix a piece of green felt to the underside, and while the glue was drying he took the necessary photographs and uploaded them to his project document. He then filled in his personal evaluation form, giving himself five out of five for all the outcomes. The only thing that could have made the finished product better, in his opinion, was to have used a nicer piece of wood. The soft pine was pithy and didn't hold a sheen that he could have achieved with something like oak or mahogany. Still, he'd made a good job of the turning and the lamp holder fitted snugly. The power cable snaked out of a neatly positioned hole. He knew it would easily pass the assessment criteria but, more importantly, he hoped Mum would be pleased with it.

He wrapped the lamp base in bubble wrap at the end of the lesson and carefully stowed it at the bottom of his backpack.

His mum *was* pleased. She was in her usual chair in the chalet and when Alex unpacked his backpack she let out an, 'Ooo. That's lovely. I'll have a look through my fabrics to make a decent shade to go with it.'

Aunty Joan was spectacularly underwhelmed by his efforts and she banged a saucepan on the stove as she added her contribution. 'You might have made something useful.'

Moth was perched with her legs under her chin on the sofa, staring intently at her phone. Alex suspected she was playing Candy Crush or some other mindless game, obviously dodging any necessity to comment on his practical skills.

And Aunty Joan was only just warming to her theme. 'Why you can't do some proper subjects at that school. Baking cakes and fiddling around with bits of wood. Where's all that going to get you?'

'I am doing Higher English.' If he could get time to read the flaming books, he wanted to add. It was difficult keeping the croft going even when Mum was functioning better. But on his own ... and having to go to school ... and trying to make much-needed cash with his fishing ...

'Well let's hope you pass.'

Alex fought the temptation to glance at Moth. Aunty Joan had allowed her to leave school with her two Higher passes in French and Geography. Proper subjects, decidedly.

They'd been to Rome once, in the October holidays, when he was still in primary school. His father was a traditional church minister in so many ways, so Daniel had been surprised when he came down for breakfast on their first morning wearing an open necked polo shirt. He looked years younger without his dog collar. His mum looked younger, too, with her spotty sundress and broad smile. Daniel had thought about that smile a lot after the holiday because she would have known, even then, that her earlier diagnosis had been way off and she only had a few months, at best, left with them.

They'd done the usual touristy things, which involved a lot of traipsing around narrow cobbled streets, and his mum had embarrassed both Daniel and his father by lingering outside a shop that sold only women's underwear. Flimsy, silky pants and bras were pegged to nylon strings in the window display. Daniel had had to grab her arm to stop her from going in.

Towards the end of the week they'd planned their tour of the catacombs. They didn't talk much as they queued with the other tourists. But when they were shunted forward in a group and were approaching the first tunnel his father had frozen. 'I'll wait for you outside,' he'd said with what could only be fear in his eyes. Mum had taken Daniel's hand and they'd walked together through to the subterranean tombs.

Daniel reached out and touched the cold stone wall beside him, wishing his mum was with him, holding his hand, right now.

CHAPTER 31

The pile of washing had finally made it from his bedroom floor to the washing machine. Alex stuffed t-shirts, socks and pants in the drum. After a moment's consideration he took off his jeans and pushed those in too. He measured out the powder and poured it in to the slide out tray.

Standing in his socks, boxers and t-shirt, he pulled Mum's apron over his head, tying the straps behind his waist. The ingredients were lined up on the kitchen table and he was pleased that they'd mostly been gathered from around the croft. There was little point using the few remaining raspberries on the canes as he couldn't commit to further batches of that. But he had a good supply of strawberries and more to come. The rowanberries from the tree beside the cattle grid were a few days off being ripe enough—he would mention rowan jelly to Tony when he took these first samples—but the brambles from behind the barn were fat and juicy. He'd had to resort to buying jam sugar at the shop—some of the fruits he'd gathered needed that extra boost of pectin. But other than that, what was left from the ten pounds Tony had given him had been sufficient to clear the outstanding phone bill. This time tomorrow the house phone should have been reconnected and he might even be in credit if the contents of his creels were everything they ought to be.

The washing machine started making a lopsided crunching noise, complaining at being overloaded. Well, he could counteract that. He sifted through Mum's pile of CDs. Definitely not Bruce Springsteen. Pink Floyd stayed in his hand for a couple of moments but then he saw the black and white cover. The synchronicity made him laugh and he slipped *In the City* by The Jam out of its sleeve, pushed it in the slot on the CD player and skipped through the tracks to Non Stop Dancing, putting it on repeat.

The jam had to be made tonight so it could set before he took it to the hotel after school. He lifted down the heavy set of cast iron scales and the large copper pan. Both had been in the croft since his great-grannie had lived here. He felt the force of his connection with these long-lived family utensils, the countless Cameron hands that had used them day after day, and along with Mum's upbeat music it helped him overcome his tiredness, despite it being well past midnight.

Fancy flavours, Tony had said. He'd get going with the rhubarb and ginger first—something he'd done before— then the mixed berries and lime. He'd bought a net of limes for fifty pence at the shop when they'd been reduced before Christmas. He'd squeezed the juice into an ice cube tray, freezing it for whenever a recipe called for that extra kick.

His feet slipped about the kitchen floor as he shuffled back from the freezer with his mugful of lime-juice ice cubes, dancing along with the track and singing out the lyrics he could remember.

The wolf whistle coincided with the break between tracks.

'Get you, hot stuff.'

Alex had locked the doors. Chuck must have come in through his bedroom window.

'Your mother's out, I guess.'

'What ... why...?' Alex couldn't form a sentence. The track started up again and Alex hit the PAUSE button.

'You need to get yourself on Bake Off dressed like that. Give the whole nation a thrill.'

Alex lined up the stems of rhubarb on the chopping board and picked up the knife to start slicing it in to chunks. 'You know, I'm a bit busy.'

'Yeah, I can see. How about I give you a hand before we go out?' Chuck let the plastic bag he was carrying drop to the floor.

'Er. No. It's all right.'

Chuck's face slid through several emotions before settling on hurt.

There was only going to be one way out of this. Jam making would have to wait until later.

'Just give me a minute. And don't touch anything.'

Alex ran upstairs and put on the trackies he'd outgrown. He'd cut the elastic at the ankles to accommodate his calf muscles but they were fine tucked in wellies out on the croft. They would have to do for now.

'What's in the bag?' he asked when he got back to the kitchen.

'It's for our picnic tonight.' Chuck took out the contents. Even lacking its head and fur, Alex could tell it was a rabbit. Freshly killed.

Chuck was unusually quiet as they left the croft and when they reached the road he turned left, up the hill, rather than right towards the village.

'Have you got somewhere in mind?' Alex asked him eventually.

Chuck's enigmatic reply was that he'd found somewhere *magical*.

But when Chuck stopped on the bridge over the river and slithered down the bank towards the rushing water, Alex's frustration overcame him. A gorge walk? In the dark?

'Fucksake, Chuck. Does everything have to be an expedition with you?'

Chuck turned an emotionless face towards him. 'Don't piss on my parade, Alex.'

Alex grunted. It was like being with a child, he realised. Chuck wanted everything his own way but needed you to be pleased about it too.

Alex followed Chuck as he clambered over boulders in the river until they reached a rockslide. Again, Chuck went on ahead, scrambling up the loose debris before pulling himself up on to a rocky ledge.

When Alex joined Chuck on the ledge he found they were facing a narrow fissure that slanted back in to the hillside for a couple of metres, making a shallow cave.

Chuck flicked his flint lighter and lit two candles that were already tucked inside the shelter of the fissure. In the middle of the rock-strewn floor was a smouldering pile of ashes.

'We're the same, you and me, Alex, aren't we?' Chuck quickly gathered a handful of dry sticks from a pile inside the fissure and pushed them in the hot ashes. 'We don't need people telling us what to do. We just get on with it—you and me.'

Alex reckoned he was right about that. He did just get on with things.

Chuck went on: 'We don't do complicated, you and me, do we? We keep things simple.'

By the time Chuck had cut the rabbit into joints with his hunting knife, flames were springing from the fire. He skewered the rabbit meat on two whittled sticks, like kebabs, and balanced them to cook over the fire.

While Chuck gave his attention to his cooking Alex found a wider part of the rocky ledge and sat down.

'So what would you do, Alex,' Chuck carried the skewers of cooked meat in one hand and sat beside Alex on the ledge, 'if some tramp turned up on your timeline claiming to be a sister?'

Alex shrugged, not knowing where Chuck was going with all this talk about family. 'You haven't got a sister then?'

Chuck let out a harsh laugh. 'No. No sister and no brother either.'

Alex tore a piece rabbit meat off his skewer with his teeth. 'But did you go to see your dad? How's he doing?'

Chuck finished chewing his own piece of meat and wiped his mouth with the back of his hand. 'Shall I tell you the truth about my dad, Alex?'

Even though he left a silent space, the way Chuck stared in to the black sky suggested he wasn't waiting an answer. 'My dad is a scumbag,' he said eventually.

This was a new twist. 'I thought you said he was a hero?'

'Oh, he is. Got the medal to prove it. That doesn't stop him being a scumbag.'

'But he's still in witness protection? He is safe?'

'I've heard he's got to be moved. Something about corrupt police. I don't even know if I should trust my liaison officer anymore. That's why I have to go back. To find out what's going on.' He handed Alex a piece of roasted rabbit. 'So this is our last supper.'

He said it all so nonchalantly. As if *witness protection* and *liaison officer* were words you used every day.

'Does your dad know where you are now? Does he know you're here?'

'Do you think a scumbag would care? As long as I turn up, if and when required, and say the right things. That's all he's concerned about.'

Alex knew from their earlier conversations that his dad was giving evidence in a case where some rogue ex-soldiers had taken the law into their own hands. But nothing more about it.

'He knows you're not at home?'

'Everybody and his lousy mother knows I'm not at home.'

Chuck picked up his hunting knife and tested the sharpness of the blade against his thumb. 'You know, Alex. There is one day, one day in your life when everything changes.'

Alex knew all about that—although he would never have stated it in such a matter-of-fact way.

'That day came early for me. Seven years old, alone, walking back from school ... scrabbling for the key under the mop bucket.'

He spoke as if he was giving a commentary on a video running in his head.

'Only able to reach the lock by upturning the bucket and standing on it ... Then the wrong smell. An acid yellow smell. You know what I mean?'

Alex didn't know, but he kept quiet.

'Even in the kitchen. Where she lay on the floor, a dribble of blood coming from the corner of her mouth. She opened her eyes and looked up. Except her left eye could only open to a tiny slit in the puffy skin surrounding it. She lifted a hand. A sweaty hand, even though it was winter and you could see your breath. "Don't wake your dad," she said before closing her eyes again.'

'So, in answer to your question. No. My hero slash scumbag of a dad has no idea where I am. And it has to stay like that. Okay?'

'I'm not about to tell anybody,' Alex said, getting the full meaning of Chuck's words.

'That's right.' Chuck wiped the blade of his knife on his combat trousers and threw it in the air, four, five times, like a juggler, catching it each time with the handle, before leaning over and placing the tip of the blade against Alex's throat.

'That should help you remember your promise,' Chuck said before closing up his knife and putting it in his trouser pocket.

FRIDAY

CHAPTER 32

There'd been a physics theory period on Thursday, so when she'd cleared away the equipment from her practical experiment Caitlin approached the teacher to find out what she'd missed.

'You feeling better today?' The teacher was new this year—straight from university.

'A bit.' There was no point in trying to make out she was fine—she knew her face told otherwise. 'Just wondering what I missed yesterday.'

The teacher opened a folder on her desk and took out a worksheet with Caitlin's name on the top.

'Thanks ... I'll take Daniel's too.'

The teacher looked flustered. 'Oh, right.' She pulled several sheets of paper from the folder until she found another copy of the worksheet.

'Maybe you could put his name on it.'

The teacher picked up her pen and did as Caitlin suggested. She seemed too embarrassed to ask about Daniel, so Caitlin told her anyway. 'There's a reconstruction tomorrow. Constable Logan said they've got a boy about the same height for it, same colour hair. It will jog people's memories. Somebody will remember seeing him.'

The teacher ran her hand through her hair. 'Yes. I'm sure,' she said, picking up a voltmeter from a desk and sloping off towards the prep room.

Alex walked around the games pitch eating the buttered bread he'd brought with him. How he'd got through the morning lessons without falling asleep or lashing out verbally at one of the teachers he didn't know. He'd never felt so tired.

After making the jam samples he'd finally got to bed around 5am. But he'd woken an hour later in a cold sweat, his duvet wrapped around him, feeling again the point of the hunting knife pressing against his throat.

Had their picnic overlooking the river gorge really been the last time he would ever see Chuck? Had he really gone for good this time?

When the bell went for afternoon lessons and the other kids made their way back to the school buildings, Alex walked out of the side gate.

On his way back to the croft he texted Moth: Meet me at boat 4:15?

She texted back her answer: Okay. Fishing? :)

He wasn't going to waste another text answering that.

If Daniel took a scrap of comfort from his surrounding it was from the smell. The blend of cold soil and hewn rock. Clean somehow. Basic. A smell that reminded him of the hours he'd spent outside as a kid, making friends with the insect life around their ramshackle home.

His incarceration was punishment for the years he'd spent being brought up in a loving family. Ellie had suffered unfathomable turmoil for most of her life. And when she'd sought him out, he'd been a patronising twat. He deserved all this.

CHAPTER 33

Alex wiped the jam jars clean and put on the decorative sticky labels he'd borrowed from the hospitality room. The bubble wrap he'd kept from when he'd brought home his table lamp—which now graced the coffee table in the living room—came in useful to protect the jars as he carefully placed them in his backpack. His favourite flavour was the strawberry and greengage, which he didn't think ought to have worked. He'd kept back a dollop in a saucer for Mum's opinion.

He reached the cove from the clifftop path feeling sure nobody had seen him. Then he rowed around the headland to the Keeper's Cottage.

Alex sincerely hoped Chuck had been telling the truth. But he needed to check with his own eyes.

Other than a few broken fronds of bracken, there was nothing to suggest Chuck had spent the last month living here. He found no trace of fire pits, no stray empty cans, no ash or charred bits of wood. And any footprints Chuck might have left in the sand had been washed away by the tide.

Satisfied that Chuck had truly gone, Alex rowed back to the cove and tied up his boat with plenty of time to get out of sight before Moth arrived to help check his creels.

He sauntered along the clifftop path and slithered down the rocky slope right on time, but Moth was already waiting for him.

'Wotcher, Faceache,' she called as he crossed the beach.

Alex smiled. Despite her being seriously annoying at times, Moth was somebody you couldn't help smiling at.

It was only when she stood up that he saw what she'd been sitting on. She held the buoyancy aid up high.

'Moth. You haven't...'

Moth looked affronted. 'Course not! Laser gave it me. He reckoned I needed a lifejacket after I told him about my near-death experience.'

'It's not a lifejacket.' Even as he said it, Alex knew his pedantry was only a cover for his own shortfall. He should have provided something to keep Moth safe. 'You could always learn to swim,' he added.

'No point ... is there? That's what Laser said.'

'There is every point! Even with one of those on.' Alex hated the received wisdom amongst fishermen that being able to swim only prolonged how long it was before you drowned if you went overboard.

'If we're going to stand here arguing all day I might as well go home.'

Alex rubbed his face with his hands, then stowed his backpack with the jam jars safely in his locker before helping Moth, now flaunting her bright orange buoyancy aid, to step over the gunwale and take her seat.

* * *

She looked like a little gnome, Alex thought as he turned the corner from the hotel kitchen. Moth was perched on the stone pillar at the end of the drive, waiting for him.

Alex took a tenner from the money Tony had given him for his catch before putting the rest in his jeans pocket. He would square up with her and, hopefully, avoid having to dish out any more loans.

On the way to the hotel she'd talked non-stop about Shane's house party in the village that night. Doubtless, her next stop before home would be at the shop.

'If you come up to the chalet after tea we can go together,' she said, jumping down from her roost to join him.

'I'm not going out tonight.'

Moth shrugged. 'Suit yourself.' She accepted the tenner from Alex without any comment. 'But you will.'

Alex's thoughts were so tangled he didn't know whether to argue with her or to laugh. There was no reason why he shouldn't go to the house party. But he had no desire to be amongst other people. He was tired. He put his bad mood down to that.

He didn't even go in the shop with Moth, just gave her a quick goodbye hug before she headed across the village green. But he'd only taken a few steps towards home when he heard the spluttering engine of a motorcycle slowing down behind him.

'Want a lift anywhere?' Angus said, letting his scooter idle as he stopped beside the kerb.

Alex shook his head.

'Okay. See you.' Angus gave him a thumbs up and Alex watched him ride around the village green and pull up outside the shop.

It was only a few minutes later that he heard the scooter on the road behind him again. This time it didn't slow down. And when it passed him, Alex saw Moth riding pillion, her hands clutching Angus' waist.

SATURDAY

CHAPTER 34

He should have had the idea. Aunty Joan had made that quite clear when she'd made it known that Caitlin had gone to the police station and demanded a reconstruction of Daniel's last known journey.

'Constable Logan would have done that anyway. She's not incompetent,' he'd said, but that didn't diminish the argument in his own head, and clearly not in Aunty Joan's, that Alex hadn't gone in demanding anything.

Caitlin was what Mum would call a doer. He'd never reflected that maybe Mum would have liked him to be more of a doer. And Caitlin couldn't be accused of not being ambitious, as Mum had hinted about him. No. Caitlin was obviously the perfect daughter, and, if Daniel's judgement was to be trusted, the perfect girlfriend too.

He arrived at the village bus stop at the time arranged and became part of the group gathered for the reconstruction: Constable Logan and a sidekick she introduced as Detective Inspector Brady—a lean bloke wearing a black suit that made him look like an undertaker; Reverend Macaulay, standing beside Eva; and a couple of journalists carrying cameras. Caitlin, with her dad in tow, was in the thick of it. She looked grim—her eyes wide open, her mouth in a straight line.

The other people, tucked in the bus shelter away from the rain, were just normal folk from the village wanting to get the early bus to town.

Alex clutched the pile of photographs Constable Logan had passed to him.

'I hope you don't mind doing this here, Alex.' Constable Logan held her umbrella over them both. 'If you could just look through them and see if you recognise anybody.'

Alex scanned the first few grainy black and white pictures that had been taken as stills from the CCTV footage at the bus station in town. They all had a date and time in the bottom right hand corner.

'No. No,' he said, fanning through the first few, but he stopped as he came to the next picture. There was Daniel, alone at the bus stance, head down and hood up so that his face was barely visible. But it was him, no doubt about it.

'You agree that is Daniel?'

Alex wished he could disagree, find something about the figure that said it wasn't Daniel. But how would that help? It wouldn't make Daniel suddenly appear at home. Where he should be.

'Yeah, it's him,' he said.

'If you wouldn't mind looking at the rest.'

Alex flicked through to the next picture.

'What is it?' Constable Logan must have caught his slight frown as he gave the picture a second glance.

'I can't be sure.'

'You recognise somebody?'

'Maybe.' Alex pointed at a figure half-turned away from the camera. A short, stocky lad wearing a baseball cap. It looked like one of Angus' goons.

'This might be a lad from school.'

'Name?' Constable Logan's voice switched from solicitous to assertive.

'George Finlayson. He was probably on the way to watch the shinty.'

'He'd be a bit early for the match though,' Constable Logan said and Alex could almost hear the cogs grinding in her head.

Alex shrugged. Wished he'd never mentioned it. 'Look. I've no idea if it is even him.'

'Don't worry. We'll check it out.'

Great. And if Angus found out Alex had landed his mate in it ...

'And did you see George there? You were playing in that match, weren't you?'

She knew very well he'd been playing. He'd already been over all that with her.

'I'm not likely to notice people in the crowd, am I?'

Constable Logan indicated for him to look through the other pictures. Some people appeared in more than one of the pictures but he didn't recognise anybody.

As Constable Logan left him alone, Caitlin's dad approached. 'Would you like a lift with us?'

'Oh...' Out of the corner of his eye, Alex saw the bus rounding the corner and the movement of the regular punters edging to the front of the bus shelter. 'No ... But thanks,' he added. 'I'll be fine.' He fished in his pocket for change to pay the driver. 'I want to take the bus. You know...'

Caitlin's dad, with his round, sad, fish eyes, turned away from him without another word.

Alex moved along the bus with the other travellers until he came to the seat he and Daniel usually sat in. He was certain Daniel would have used this seat last week.

Where were you going, Daniel? What the fuck were you doing?

About a mile from town the bus began to slow down. Alex glanced through the window, past the raindrops that made random patterns on the glass like the dot to dot puzzles he'd enjoyed as a kid, and took a sharp intake of breath. Standing at the back of the bus shelter they were approaching was Daniel. Beside him stood Constable Logan and DI Brady and behind them a couple of blokes with cameras hanging around their necks.

No. It wasn't Daniel. The boy was the same height and had a wiry frame like Daniel's. He was dressed in the same style of hoodie and jeans that Daniel wore, but his black hair was cut short, whereas Daniel's always flopped about like a mop head. Alex breathed again.

As the bus came to a halt, the boy pulled up his hood and stepped on to the bus. He didn't pay any fare but walked up the central aisle with a confident swagger that would have set him apart from Daniel in a moment.

Behind the boy, one of the journalists got on the bus too. And as the bus pulled away Alex turned to watch Constable Logan and DI Brady stride back to the police van that was parked at the rear of the bus bay.

They were all at the bus stance: the two police officers standing beside Reverend Macaulay; Eva with a handkerchief in her fist; Caitlin and her dad. The few journalists who'd been at the village had been joined by more from town. From his seat by the window, Alex saw a couple of them mucking about, laughing and joking, oblivious to the distress being felt by the people who knew and loved Daniel.

The boy who wasn't Daniel remained in his seat until all the other punters, Alex included, had left the bus. Eva spotted Alex and she beckoned him over. She put her arm around his shoulder and pulled him into a hug.

Alex saw that a video camera, set up on a tripod, was focused on the front of the bus. DI Brady indicated that the filming should commence and the boy stepped off the bus.

Constable Logan bent to speak to Eva. 'We've talked to everybody round and about this morning and the video will go out on TV this evening.'

Reverend Macaulay thanked her. Eva was incapable of speech.

As if on cue, DI Brady smoothed down his hair and walked in front of the camera. He began to speak in a clear, deep voice. 'Daniel has not been in contact with his family or friends since Friday evening, and so far we have been unable to establish his current whereabouts.'

Alex missed the next part of the Inspector's speech due to Eva's sobs into her handkerchief.

'As such, we are keen to hear from anyone who believes they have seen him since then and would urge anyone with information to contact the police immediately. In addition, I would ask Daniel to get in touch and let us know he is safe and well,' DI Brady concluded.

Off-camera now, DI Brady instructed the boy who wasn't Daniel to walk in different directions away from the bus stance—along the road into town, which was the route it was thought Daniel had taken; then along the road in the other direction, towards the industrial estate, in case Daniel had switched direction after being caught by the CCTV camera; and finally towards the pedestrian underpass to the train station.

'He's not walking right,' Alex said but nobody paid him any attention.

And then it was all over. The journalists started packing away their equipment and the crowd began to disperse.

'I'll be waiting for the next few buses to come in and we'll question the passengers,' Constable Logan said to Reverend Macaulay. 'If Daniel had been waiting around for a while, somebody who comes into town regularly might have seen him.'

Alex knew the police were doing all they could. But it wasn't enough. Nobody had seen Daniel for a whole week. All those days had passed by and Daniel was still missing.

MONDAY

CHAPTER 35

There were no other students at the computers. Pushing aside the chairs so that they could both view the screen, Alex logged on to a computer in the furthest corner from the door. Angus stood close beside him. Alex noticed his brilliant white polo shirt and that citrusy aftershave. Maybe Angus was always careful about his appearance and their encounter at the croft had really just been a wind up after all.

Alex took a slight step to the side, away from Angus, and leaned on the computer bench—but Angus closed the gap and leaned in too. If anything, they were now even closer, their cheeks just centimetres apart as they stared at the screen.

'You can't deny it forever, you know.' Angus' voice was a low murmur.

Alex didn't want this conversation. Not now and certainly not with Angus. He felt his neck redden and he pointed to the screen. 'It's all here.' Yet again, Alex had been singled out to help Angus catch up. 'You know what to do.'

'Yeah. I do.' The innocuous sounding comment was embellished with a grin.

Alex turned his eyes studiously towards the screen. 'You've got it wrong, you know. Got me wrong.'

'If you say so.'

Alex was nettled by Angus' self-assurance. 'You think you know me better than I know myself?'

'You can be confused, uncertain even, until something like this happens.' Angus slid his hand over Alex's right buttock and gave it a gentle squeeze.

Alex's cock didn't actually stiffen but he felt the tingle in his balls.

'Now. Tell me you would rather a girl had done that. Any girl.'

'It's really none of your business.'

'Point taken.' Angus pushed a chair behind Alex's knees and Alex toppled into the seat. Angus wheeled him into position at the computer then pulled up another chair for himself. 'So. You going to get me started?'

Alex was relieved to hear that Angus was now referring to the task in hand.

She didn't want to approach him. The way he hunkered in the corner of the canteen as if he wanted the walls to swallow him up suggested he wouldn't welcome the interruption. But she had to.

He didn't look up, even though she was standing so close to him there could be no mistaking her intention.

'Alex,' she said eventually.

Still no response.

She launched straight in. 'I've had a text from Daniel.'

Alex's head snapped up. 'Show me.'

Who did he think he was? Telling her what to do. 'He said to tell you he's all right.'

Alex stood up and even with his stooped shoulders he towered over her. 'Let me see.'

There were just the four words. But she fumbled in her bag for her phone and opened the message. She passed the phone to Alex and watched him read the words that she'd memorised: Tell Alex I'm OK.

Alex took a quick look then passed the phone back to her. 'It's not from Daniel.'

It seemed there would be no further discussion on the matter.

'How?'

Alex had already slumped back in his seat but turned his face towards her. 'It doesn't sound like him.'

He was jumping to conclusions. He had no reason to say it. But something similar had crossed her mind too. She'd been so excited to see a message from Daniel show up on her phone that, initially, her usual powers of deduction had deserted her. She'd yelled out loud thinking Daniel was alive.

But on her way to the canteen to find Alex she'd considered a number of scenarios behind the message: Daniel had gone off wild camping and had only just found somewhere to charge his phone; he'd lost his phone while doing something—Caitlin couldn't think what—and now he'd found it. Or maybe he'd wanted to keep his whereabouts secret but he knew people would be worried and he'd sent the message to reassure everyone. At least the message meant that Daniel hadn't had an accident and his body wasn't lying broken at the bottom of a cliff or something similar.

A less benign scenario wouldn't be denied head space: Daniel had lost his phone and some sicko had found it and sent the message.

She'd asked herself other questions too. Why had Daniel sent the message to her rather than directly to Alex? Yet Daniel had mentioned how haphazard Alex was with his phone—always losing it, never remembering to charge it. And why—why—no message for her?

Now here was Alex, looking dishevelled and worn out, adding his own succinct reflection on the veracity of the message and giving her reason for further turmoil.

Whatever was going on she couldn't lose the plot now. The next thing she must do was get her phone, with its debatable message, to Constable Logan.

At last the bell sounded for the end of the school day. Alex was already waiting by the English classroom door, his bag slung over one shoulder. He was out of the building before the reverberations from the ringing had left his ears.

His "to do" list was still the same. Get Mum home and find Daniel. He'd spent most of Sunday with Mum at the chalet and, finally, he reckoned Aunty Joan was reaching the conclusion that Mum going home would be beneficial to her recovery. An opinion that had seemed cemented when Mum leaned over to Alex and said, as she thought conspiratorially, yet Alex knew Aunty Joan's earflaps were wagging, 'I wish I was at home. I'm missing the hens.'

Alex hadn't taken advantage of the comment there and then. He knew Aunty Joan would only come back with some counter argument if he pushed it. Better to let Aunty Joan think it was her own idea for Mum to go home.

Wrapped in his own thoughts, Alex didn't see Angus standing on the pavement beside his scooter until he was almost alongside him. Alex didn't even so much as flick a recognition in Angus' direction. But it didn't seem to matter. Angus fell in step, pushing his scooter along the road, as Alex hurried along the pavement.

'Fucksake, Angus. What is it?'

'Wondered if you'd like to hang out later?'

'I'm sort of busy today.'

'Thought you might welcome some company. With Daniel ... You know.'

Alex quickened his step. 'You've got this all wrong. Really. I don't need company.'

'Just trying to help.'

Alex came to a sudden halt. 'I don't need *helping*.' His voice raised a few semitones making the syllables sound strangled. 'I'm not some saddo who can't—'

'Hey. Not so serious, bud. It's no big deal.'

How did Angus manage to look so laid back just standing on the pavement? Alex took a deep breath. And when he said, 'What's with all the concern, anyway?' he was glad his voice had returned to its normal register. He went on, 'Surely you don't want to ruin your tough-guy reputation.' That ought to be enough to get rid of him.

But to Alex's surprise, Angus laughed. 'Quite an act, heh? The kids should think themselves lucky me and my mates are positioned at the top of the stinking pile. Could be someone with a nasty streak otherwise.'

Alex allowed a reluctant smile to crack his face at this admission. 'Very public spirited of you.'

Angus smiled back, a full beefy smile, and Alex felt his gut churn.

'Och well.' Angus held out a slip of paper. 'Here's my number. Text me.'

As Alex unlocked the back door he could see Stewart's car approaching on the single-track road. He just had time to pick up the rag doll that was spread-eagled on the gravel—this one looked a bit worse for wear—before Stewart's car rumbled over the cattle grid.

From where he was standing, Alex could see two people in the back seats. Aunty Joan got out first then scooted around the back of the vehicle to help Mum out.

Mum stood for a moment, feet together, arms by her side. Stewart lifted her small flowery case from the boot and passed it to Aunty Joan. Taking a step towards the house Mum wafted a hand in front of her face, batting away the cloud of midges that was gathering around the car.

'Come on then,' Aunty Joan said to nobody in particular. And they all trooped indoors.

Aunty Joan wasn't going to be accused of showing approval, but neither did she make any disparaging remarks. Alex took note of the way her eyes scanned the kitchen. 'I think your mother would like a cup of tea,' she said eventually. 'I'll take this upstairs.'

Stewart pulled out a chair from under the kitchen table for Mum to sit down. She laid her skinny arms across the table top and when Alex put her favourite mug in front of her with tea made just the way she liked it, she looked up at him and said, 'That's better.'

It was all Alex needed to hear.

'The flowers upstairs need some water,' Aunty Joan said as she strode back into the kitchen. Then, 'Come on Stewart. Everything's in order. I need to get back for my four-thirty appointment.'

Stewart swallowed the mouthful of tea he had just taken, rinsed his mug in the sink and placed it on the drainer. 'See you later, Cath,' he said, giving Mum a kiss on the cheek. 'And good luck,' he said to Alex.

With their leaving, Alex felt happier than he had for a long time. This was the place he wanted to be: with Mum, in their kitchen.

The rumble on the cattle grid was too soon for Stewart and Aunty Joan to be going out, nor was it the right sound for the Nissan. His heart began to beat faster as he looked out of the window and watched the police van pull up. Stewart and Aunty Joan remained seated in their car as Constable Logan and DI Brady got out of their vehicle.

'Stay here,' Alex said to Mum as he left the kitchen.

Constable Logan must have some news of Daniel, Alex reckoned as he opened the door to the police officers. And judging by the expression on her face, the news wasn't good.

CHAPTER 36

They trooped into the village police station, Constable Logan leading the way and DI Brady bringing up the rear. Alex was shepherded towards a table beside the window, although with the blind fully closed there was no view out of, nor into, the room. Alex sat at one side of the table and Constable Logan at the other. DI Brady sifted through papers on a messy work desk in the centre of the room before joining them, sitting beside Constable Logan.

'What's going on? I thought ... you had some news of Daniel.'

Constable Logan ignored his comment. Alex got the message from her body language; she was the one who would be asking the questions. She placed her elbows on the table and clasped her hands in front of her. 'Alex. I know you've not been telling me the truth about a few things.'

Alex hesitated. If this wasn't about Daniel, he wasn't going to deny or admit anything until he'd heard more.

'And so I've asked you to come here, voluntarily, so that I can ask you some questions.' She paused. 'I want you to answer me truthfully. Do you understand?'

Alex nodded. He felt like a six-year-old being told off by an odious head teacher.

'Because, unless you convince me otherwise, I have suspicions that you might have committed an offence.' She leaned forward to underline the seriousness of her comment.

'No. Really. I—'

'I'm now going to tell you about rights you have as a suspect. Please listen carefully.'

A suspect? Alex did listen carefully. He didn't want his stay extended by needing to have things said twice. He heard clearly that his rights included him having access to a solicitor. He intimated, just as clearly, that he didn't want that. Then he answered 'yes' when asked if he understood that he could change his mind if he wanted to.

'I just want to get back to Mum. She'll be—'

'I know, Alex. So let's get this sorted out now, shall we?' Constable Logan signed some forms and passed them to DI Brady to sign too.

'First of all, I want to thank you for giving your DNA sample the other day.'

Constable Logan looked directly at him, but DI Brady seemed more interested in the posters on the walls.

'The jumper did indeed have your DNA on it, as we thought it might. Didn't we?'

'I said mine was missing.'

'You did. Thing is, our forensics team also found other evidence of your DNA at the scene where the body was found.'

Was that all? 'I keep my boat there. I'm up and down that stretch of beach nearly every other day.'

'You are. So when we found a patch of blood not far from the body, that proved to be yours from the tests run on it, well, I said to DI Brady here,' she glanced at Brady but he was still staring at the walls, 'that you could have cut yourself at any time.'

Alex narrowed his eyes. The blood must have been from where he'd fallen over the pile of seaweed. Right next to the body. He fought the temptation to touch his forehead where the graze from his fall had now all but healed over.

'Except the blood was *barely dry*, so our crime team reported,' Constable Logan unclasped her fingers and placed her hands, palm down, on the table. 'And what we also found, close to the body, was somebody's breakfast that they'd not been able to keep in their stomach.'

Alex struggled to remain impassive.

'Mrs Macgregor, who, as you know, found the body, assured us she hadn't vomited at the scene.'

DI Brady was still examining the walls.

'Did you find the body, Alex? Was it your breakfast that wouldn't stay down?'

DI Brady's gaze shifted from the walls to inspect Alex's face.

Alex nodded.

Constable Logan let out a sigh. 'Will you confirm that for me, Alex.'

'Yes. I found the body. I went to check my boat the morning after the storm and the body was there on the beach.'

'Thanks for clearing that up. There's just a few more questions before we can think about letting you go.'

Think about letting him go! He needed better than that.

'I panicked,' he said. And he went on to tell them how it had been when he'd found the body. He told them how anxious Daniel had been to get to school on time, that there was no phone signal on the beach. He explained that Daniel hadn't gone with him down to the cove and Alex was the only one who'd seen the body.

'But you didn't phone anybody when you got to school? The police for instance? Isn't that what anybody would have done?'

Alex shrugged. It sounded pathetic, he knew. But he hadn't done anything wrong by not phoning.

Alex looked at the clock on the wall. It had been twenty minutes since Constable Logan had started her questions.

'I'm still not buying this, Alex,' she said.

They'd been going around in circles but he stuck to his story. He'd lent his jumper to a wild camper. He'd seen the lad a few times since, he knew his name was Chuck but nothing else for sure about him, and yes, he had been stupid not to phone the police when he'd found the body. He hadn't a clue who the girl was or how she'd got the jumper. He'd just freaked out when he'd found the body because he thought it was Chuck and he didn't want to get involved. Didn't want his mum getting worried.

'But why, Alex, would you not want your mum to know you'd been involved with this camper ... this, Chuck ... if you had nothing to hide?'

'She's not been well.'

'You've told us. But I'm still not convinced.'

It was a stalemate. Alex had to tell her something otherwise he'd be here all evening.

He took a deep breath. 'He—Chuck—ran short of cash. I sort of helped him when he needed food.'

'I assume when you say "helped" you mean nicked stuff?'

Alex nodded.

'Do you make a habit of taking things that don't belong to you then?'

'No. Never. Not before—'

'And yet you felt it was okay to "help" out this random wild camper, who you'd only seen a couple of times, by stealing things?' She put her hands behind her head and leaned back in her seat. 'Was he bullying you?'

Too far. She was pushing too far.

'No. Nothing like that ... but ... we'd done a few crazy things that I didn't want people knowing about.'

'He was blackmailing you?'

'No. No.'

DI Brady walked across to a desk in the centre of the room and opened a drawer. When he returned to his place at the table he unfolded a map of the area and spread it in front of Alex. 'Show us where he's camping.'

Alex screwed up his eyes. He shook his head. 'He's not there anymore.'

'That may be the case, Alex,' Constable Logan said. 'But at the moment, all we've got is your DNA at a crime scene where there was a suspicious death. If you don't want to be charged with being involved with that death, we need to check out what you're telling us.'

'And I want you to shut the fuck up with your whingeing on about getting home to your mam,' added DI Brady. 'A lassie's body, wearing your jumper, was found where you keep your boat, with your blood and vomit near to her. So if you don't tell us all you know, I'll be arresting you.'

He had no choice—he had to get home to Mum. He ran his index finger over the map until he reached the site of the Keeper's Cottage. 'It was in the ravine behind the cottage.'

Constable Logan refolded the map so that the Keeper's Cottage and the coast around it could be viewed. 'Thanks for that, Alex. That will do for now. Anything else you think of, let us know.'

'But what about ... I thought you had news about Daniel.'

'Not unless you have anything to tell us?' Constable Logan was busy sliding the map into a plastic bag but stopped to look up at him. 'I did wonder, though, why you told Caitlin the text she received today wasn't from Daniel.'

'It didn't sound like him.'

'Yes. Caitlin told us. What made you say that?'

Then Alex realised what it was that had bothered him about the message. 'He would never use OK. Even in a text. He hates it.'

'Right. Thanks. That could be helpful.'

Alex paced to the office door, eager to get away.

'Oh, by the way.' DI Brady looked up from his desk where he was staring at the screen and clicking his mouse. 'How well did Daniel know this Chuck?'

'Not at all, really.'

'Daniel wasn't with you on the occasions you met up with him then?'

'Sometimes.'

'I think you should have told us all this before. Don't you?'

He ran all the way back to the croft, pausing only when he needed to take deep breaths to combat the stitch in his side. He hurtled up the path to the back door but checked his pace as he entered the small lobby.

The croft was in silence. He opened the kitchen door and peered in. Nobody there. He hurried upstairs. Nobody.

He hurtled down stairs and stormed into Mum's workroom. Nothing. Nobody. Back in the kitchen he glared out of the window to the garden beyond. The whole croft was empty apart from his own pitiful presence.

Anger tracked through his veins. His head was about to explode.

He seized the mug Stewart had left on the drainer and pitched it at the wall. It smashed into tiny shards that clinked as they hit the worktop and chinked when they hit the floor.

He grabbed Mum's favourite mug from where it had been left on the table. His hand hovered for a fraction of a second and then he threw that too. It ricocheted off the cupboard, splashing the remains of the tea up the wall, and landed at his feet, intact apart from the handle, which had broken off in one piece, making a question mark by his toes. Not daring to touch it again, he left it, accusing him, on the floor.

He placed his hands on the worktop, oblivious of the splinters stabbing his palms, and smacked his forehead against the wall cupboard again and again.

But the physical pain couldn't combat the echoes of darkness: the low keening from the women as he helped shoulder Dad's coffin out of the church; the stifled sobs from Mum's bedroom he was never able to do anything about; and his own silent rage, trapped in his head in his struggle to 'be brave'.

He was out of his depth. With nobody to go to for help.

He turned on the cold tap full blast, splashed water on his face, then picked up the keys to the Corsa van.

The tyres threw up gravel as Alex pushed the accelerator pedal to the floor. He headed away from the village, screeching around the hairpin bends that led up the hillside.

A young deer stepping out in front of him made him hit the brakes hard and the Corsa skidded on the loose stones at the side of the road. The van turned through 180 degrees and Alex found himself facing back the way he'd come. Panting heavily, he loosened his grip on the steering wheel. He stared ahead at the dwellings ribboned along the river, dotted sparsely up here, but huddled together in the shelter of the lower glen where the river met the sea, the evening sunlight flooding the scene with an orange glow.

This was his landscape. Never before had he hated it so much.

CHAPTER 37

Caitlin knocked on the back door of the croft house one more time. No way was she taking any more of Alex's evasiveness. She was going to tackle him about what it was he was hiding.

In her frustration, she pushed down on the door handle, intending to open the door a chink and call out Alex's name, but the door was locked.

So ... neither Alex nor his mum were at home. She backed away and scanned the outside of the house. The downstairs windows at the back were all closed, but an upper window was open, possibly the bathroom judging by its frosted glass. As she walked around the side of the building she noticed that another window, the one above the stick-shed, was ajar too.

She knew she should just collect her bike and go home— but a compost bin made a handy step to climb onto the shed roof. As she clambered up, keeping her balance surprisingly easily on the gentle slope of the corrugated tin, Caitlin found herself peering into what could only be Alex's bedroom. She didn't hesitate. Even though it was stiff on its sash cords, she managed to push the window up a few more centimetres and she shoogled herself through the gap.

The enormity of what she'd done hit her as she stood at the foot of Alex's bed, but she had to act. She had so many questions; she needed to find some sort of answers. Because, meanwhile, the rest of the world was slipping back into normality; they'd even started up after-school activities again today. Yet for Caitlin, Daniel's absence had created a hole right in the centre of her, so enormous she would never have believed it possible before she'd met him.

The house had its own sounds, as well as those that came in from outdoors, the chooks gathering around their henhouse ready to be closed in for the evening, the wind swooshing through the Sitka spruce plantation on the hill behind the croft, but Caitlin listened carefully for any signs to indicate human activity. She took a step out of Alex's room and stood for a moment on the square landing, still listening. Confident there was nobody home, she made a quick tour of the house before returning to the bedroom and closing the door behind her.

Next to Alex's bed was a small wood-effect desk. She tried to open the desk drawer but that was locked. The computer was the obvious first place to investigate. She switched on and a screen saver of an outboard motor sprang into view. She clicked a few keys. 'No password, Alex. Very remiss of you. But thank you,' she muttered to herself as she opened his internet browser. She was here to get information out of Alex. Maybe it was fortunate he was out. She might find out more without him.

Caitlin wasn't a girl who was easily shocked, but she felt herself blush when she scanned the list of recent sites Alex had visited. However, she considered, that was Alex's personal business. Could it possibly have affected Daniel in any way? She didn't imagine so.

She resisted the temptation to explore his use of strategy in League of Legends.

She found that Alex hardly ever used his email account and there was little of interest there. The only recent emails he'd received were a few payment notifications from PayPal.

She rattled the locked drawer again. There had to be something in there he needed to keep secret. She began her search for the key, scanning the room for likely hiding places. The room was so unlike her own, purposeful bedroom. Yet it wasn't just that it was a boy's room, she got the sense that its occupant was barely surviving in here.

That there had been a recent attempt to clean the room was obvious. There was a tidemark in the dust on the top of the set of drawers where somebody had swept a cloth around the haphazardly placed items. She knelt on what once would have been a brightly coloured rag-rug and looked under the bed, giving her eyes time to adjust to the lower light level. A wooden box had been pushed up against the wall. She stretched her arm through the dust balls and retrieved the box but was reluctant to open it.

It looked private, intimate. But she needed to find the desk drawer key.

The contents of the box were nothing of note. Some articles cut from the local paper—Caitlin didn't have time to give them more than a cursory glance – and a few old photographs, some of them clearly of Alex with both his parents. Another showed younger versions of Alex and Daniel standing holding a huge silver cup between them—broad grins on their faces. But there was no key.

Caitlin replaced the box and stood next to the bed. Her father's voice came to her with his annoying phase he always spouted forth when she had a problem she couldn't solve: "Look outside the box, Caitlin." She gave a small laugh at the irony of it now, then stepped up onto the chair she'd been sitting on at the desk to get a new perspective on the room. "Thanks, Dad," she said as she saw the small key balanced on top of the doorframe.

She arranged the items from the drawer on the desk in front of her. A webcam, a black curly wig and a telephone bill showing an overdue account and a few scribbled amounts crossed out.

CHAPTER 38

Alex drove down to the village at a steady speed and took the turning to the chalet. He parked halfway up the track and walked the remaining distance. No point in antagonising Aunty Joan any further. He was almost at their gate when his aunt appeared.

'They let you out then?'

'What do you mean? Of course they—'

'I've told you before. That innocent look doesn't work on me. I knew you were involved in something. And let me tell you, if you've done anything to hurt Daniel...'

How could she even think such a thing?

'Are you crazy?'

Aunty Joan looked shocked. A deep frown crossed her forehead. 'Your mother is in there asleep. She needed more medication than I would have liked her to take before she calmed down ... after you were taken—'

'The police only wanted my help, since you're asking.'

'Help that you couldn't give them at home.'

There was no reasoning with her. And if Mum was asleep, medicated even, he wasn't going to disturb her.

'This isn't finished,' he said through tight lips. As he turned to go he caught sight of Moth at the chalet window but she backed away when she saw him looking. It was like that, then, was it?

There was never any traffic on the approach to the croft and Alex steered the Corsa van with confidence, holding his speed around the blind corners even with the setting sun hitting him full on the face. It was as he came out of one of the bends that he saw it ahead: a motorbike of some description, heading full pelt towards him. He managed to slow the van a little, and the rider tried to swerve out of the way, so that when the collision happened—the bike sliding against the front of the van—the rider rolled across the bonnet before hitting the ground. Alex killed the engine and rushed to where the rider had landed in a screwed-up ball in the grass.

'Are you all right? Can you hear me?'

The rider twisted around and pulled himself into a sitting position.

'Are you all right?' Alex repeated. 'Shall I call an ambulance?'

The rider shook his head slightly as he took off his helmet, revealing his identity. 'I'll be fine in a bit,' Angus said. 'How's the scooter?'

Alex stopped staring at Angus to glance over to where the Lambretta lay. He helped Angus to his feet and then lifted the scooter, with a few dents in its side to show for the collision, on to its stand.

'It doesn't look too bad.' Alex reckoned the scooter had fared better than the Corsa van, which had gained a new shaped bonnet and lost a wing mirror.

'Thought I'd find out why you hadn't texted me,' Angus said from where he was sprawled on the sofa with his leather jacket behind his head.

It felt like an age since Angus had pressed his phone number into Alex's palm outside school. 'It's like I said. I'm a bit busy this evening.'

'You certainly seem in a rush. So...' Angus got up and slung his jacket over his shoulders. 'I'll let you get on.'

'Oh. If you're all right ... I'll see you around.' Alex picked up the helmet from the coffee table with both hands and held it towards Angus.

Angus' hands were warm and firm where they covered Alex's own. And the kiss was light and tender, full on his lips. Alex fought a craving to return the kiss. But then it was all over anyway.

'Okay. See you.' Angus said as he headed towards the back door.

'Okay.' The word was barely a whisper as it left his mouth. Yet maybe it was the answer. 'Okay,' he said again, a little more confidently.

Angus turned back to look at him. 'Is everything all right. You're not—'

'I'm probably completely wrong.'

Angus dipped his eyebrows, puzzled.

'It's just that word. Okay,' Alex tried to explain. 'It's given me an idea. Can I have a lift?'

Angus shrugged. 'Sure. Where do you want to go?'

'I'll be with you in a minute.' It was a long shot. And probably too ridiculous. But it was something he had to follow up. Maybe that text *had* been from Daniel. And maybe it held a clue.

He charged up to his bedroom, struggled his way into a jumper, dropped his binoculars into his backpack, then hurried back downstairs.

'It might be a bit rough going,' Alex said, putting on his jacket.

'Never usually a problem,' Angus said with a grin.

When Caitlin witnessed the two boys entering the croft, seeing Angus push the scooter up the track followed by Alex driving the van, instead of panicking she quickly replaced the items in the desk drawer and stole across the landing to enter the other bedroom, sliding behind the door, which was the only place to hide should anyone come in. She listened to the murmur of their voices, holding her breath when she heard footsteps thumping up the stairs and then, thankfully, soon after, down. She heard the voices pick up again, although she couldn't hear what was being said. Then she heard the back door closing and the sound of the scooter engine fading away as it left the croft.

She had no way of knowing if Alex was still downstairs. After what must have been a good ten minutes or more, during which time she hadn't heard any noises at all,

Caitlin ventured through all the rooms again to check there really was nobody at home.

The light was fading, but back in Alex's bedroom she was reluctant to switch on the bedside lamp. The glow from the computer screen only served to emphasise the surrounding gloom. She'd made a stab at what Alex had been up to with his curly wig, and another quick check through the recent websites he'd visited confirmed her suspicions. She still didn't think it had anything to do with Daniel's disappearance and her next line of enquiry was to investigate further the inner world of Alex's computer.

She struggled at first—not knowing what, if anything, she was pursuing. She closed her eyes and made a mental list, an order of procedure. With systematic probing, it wasn't long before she found the hidden email account. That Alex's computer had been hacked wasn't open to doubt. Maybe Caitlin wasn't the only person who'd found it easy to get into Alex's bedroom when the house was empty.

Bizarrely, she found someone had recently ordered a second-hand physics revision book from this hidden account to be delivered to a collection point in town. She was shocked to see it was the title that had been dropped off at her house. Could it have been someone other than Daniel who had left it in their porch? She'd been so righteous in reprimanding Alex and his lack of security she hadn't considered her own safe world might have been breached. She thought back. The boy in the woods with the ostentatious earring? Had he anything to do with all this?

Instead of getting answers, she was unearthing more and more questions.

Scrolling through the messages, she found that this same account had been used, almost exclusively, by someone going by the name of Ellie.

The first message was dated about ten days ago, although it looked as if it was mid-conversation. There were a number of replies from Daniel too. Obviously, someone had used this hidden account to access Daniel's messaging. The final email from Ellie was to arrange a meeting with Daniel last Saturday.

Caitlin concluded that Daniel had gone off to Perth to meet somebody. Somebody possibly called Ellie—apparently claiming to be Daniel's twin sister. And with this Ellie insisting on such secrecy it was no wonder he hadn't mentioned it to her—or Alex.

She reached into her jeans pocket to take a picture of the screen with her phone. Shit. Constable Logan had asked her to leave her mobile with them so that they could try a trace on the text message. She would have to use the house phone downstairs to contact the police.

It wasn't a satisfactory conversation when she eventually got through to emergency services. She left a message for Constable Logan with the control room, hoping rather than being convinced that the message would be relayed with the urgency she'd demanded.

After leaving the croft, the scooter turned on to the single-track lane up the hill and then on to the old Coffin

Road—the route linking the croft to the Old Manse, which Alex and Daniel had used thousands of times when they were younger.

The surface of the track was reasonably well-kept and Angus had no difficulty avoiding the occasional ruts and potholes. Angus pulled up when Alex tapped him on the shoulder as they rounded the hilltop. There was a good view of the surroundings from this point.

Alex took out the binoculars he'd put in his backpack. As he'd suspected, he could see a police van snaking along the coastline track that eventually ended at the Keeper's Cottage. They weren't wasting any time checking out his story. But it was time they should have spent looking for Daniel. Let's face it, he reasoned, the girl they'd found was dead. She couldn't be helped any more, whereas Daniel...

Alex couldn't bring himself to believe anything other than that Daniel was alive somewhere, waiting for him.

Pressing on with their journey, Angus slowed the scooter as they passed by the lochan in the woods where the Coffin Road dwindled into no more than a stony path. He stopped beside the gate to the graveyard.

The overhanging trees sliced the early evening light into quivering fingers as Alex dismounted.

'And you don't want to tell me what this is all about?'

Alex hadn't a clue what he might find here, if anything. Reverend Macaulay had made a point of searching all the dusty rooms in the Old Manse when Daniel had first gone missing. This was probably just another of his senseless hunches. He shook his head.

'See you tomorrow then.'

'Aye. See you tomorrow.'

Alex watched Angus navigate his scooter around to the front of the church, holding up his hand in the air for a goodbye wave, before hitting the main road to the village.

With his trainers soaking up rainwater from the grassy path, Alex approached the Old Manse. Despite the fact that Alex had loved his visits here as a kid, he'd been glad when, following the death of his wife, Reverend Macaulay had moved with Daniel to the village. With the closing up of the house, painful recollections had been boxed away and left behind with the outmoded furnishings.

The imposing oak front door was stiff on its hinges but, with a shove, it opened without a sound.

It had been the "OK" in the text sent from Daniel's phone that had led him here, but if Alex needed any further sign that something not right was going on it was there in front of him. Hanging by its hand caught in the closed vestibule door was one of Mum's rag dolls—the purple paisley patterned dress now a muddy brown, the cheery face covered in a dried green slime.

The work of a wide-ranging fox? No way could he believe that.

Were the dolls another sort of coded message to him? If they were, it was lost on him; something else his brain couldn't compute.

Or was he just being an irrational prat, making up theories and stories where none existed?

He opened the glass-panelled door and released the doll, brushed off the worst of the grime, then stepped into the gloomy hallway with its stink of neglect.

CHAPTER 39

She didn't know where Angus had gone when he'd left the croft, maybe taking Alex with him on his scooter, but she'd been to a couple of parties at his house in the village. Caitlin picked up her bike from where she'd dropped it beside the hedge and set off.

He was probably the last person she should be approaching. Before this evening, the last time she'd seen Alex and Angus together they'd been tearing lumps out of each other. But she'd heard no raised voices downstairs in the house, no sounds of fighting. She had to find out if he knew anything.

As she freewheeled her bike through the village she saw Angus' scooter parked up by the side of his house. It was getting dark and a light above the front door flicked on as she approached. Angus' father answered the door and when she said she wanted to see Angus he ushered Caitlin into a narrow hallway that smelled of cats.

From the wood-panelled hall, Alex turned first to the kitchen. Mrs Macaulay had made this the hub of the home.

It was in here that she'd regularly challenged Alex and Daniel on their choice of words as they sat together at the kitchen table writing their primary school weekly diaries. The term "OK" had never been allowed. Even the less offensive "all right" had made her cheeks shiver with disgust.

If the text *was* a message from Daniel, then surely this was the place he had wanted to lead him.

Alex scanned the room, ran a hand over the cooking range which rust was beginning to claim, opened doors on built-in cupboards. All empty. Disused.

Seemed like he was being an irrational prat after all. The rest of the house would be the same: dark, gloomy, soulless.

Leaving the kitchen to its dust and memories Alex moved across the hall to the drawing room. He halted at the open door, still wary, alert, then stepped into the vast, empty space. His trainers made soft squeaks on the polished wood floor as he crossed the room.

He took a seat in the corner of the bay window, leaned back against the faded velvet curtains, then took out his binoculars and gave a careful sweep of the gardens and the land beyond. Nothing out of the ordinary.

He climbed the wide staircase and paused for a moment on the halfway landing to get a view from the window there, but the coloured glass panels made it difficult to see anything other than a blurred impression of the overgrown kitchen garden at the rear of the house.

Making his way along the upstairs hallway, he glanced briefly into the empty bedrooms opening on either side.

Reverend Macaulay's office had been a box room at the end of the hallway. The door was closed and when Alex tried the handle, he found it was locked. After three attempts to force the door open with his shoulder, it gave way with a splintering crack and Alex tumbled forwards.

An imposing desk had once taken centre stage in the room, but Alex knew that piece of furniture was now adding grandeur to the reverend's new office in the village. What he saw in its place here was a rickety trestle table. And on the table, its screen open but facing away from him, was a laptop. The laptop was plugged into a multi-socket trailing lead, which, Alex reckoned, could be powered, when needed, by the generator on the floor.

Alex swivelled around when he heard the voice behind him.

'You made it then. Perfect timing too.'

'What the fuck are you doing here?' Alex said, dropping the rag doll to the floor.

CHAPTER 40

That his wrists were tied together behind him became clear as Alex regained consciousness on the dusty floor. He tried to stand but his legs were bound together too, just above his knees. The stinging at the back of his throat was a reminder of his shock when Chuck, with a sweep of his arm, had knocked him off balance and pressed a cloth over his face.

In his tribal patterned swim shorts, a skin-tight white t-shirt and wearing thin blue latex gloves, Chuck was gathering the laptop from the trestle table and stowing it in a camouflage rucksack.

'Daniel?' Alex's voice came out as a thick growl. 'Where is he?'

'Oh, he's OK.' Chuck emphasised the last word before casting Alex a supercilious smile and leaving the room.

Alex manoeuvred himself into a sitting position, his head pounding with each slight movement. He managed to shuffle along a little way on his bottom towards the door. What the fuck was going on?

Alex heard footsteps; then Chuck, carrying a bulging plastic shopping bag, came back into the room.

'Don't worry. It won't be long now.' Chuck patted Alex on the head as he pushed past him. 'A little party first.'

Alex watched Chuck unpack the contents of the shopping bag. First out were several large candles that he distributed around the room: some on the floor, a couple on the mantelpiece and one on the deep window seat. Next were two plastic picnic tumblers and a half empty bottle of vodka.

Chuck poured vodka into one of the tumblers and crossed over to Alex. Grabbing hold of Alex's hair, Chuck forced Alex's head back and poured the vodka into his mouth. A quick clasp around Alex's wrist and Chuck had folded the tumbler into Alex's right hand. Then he crossed to the window, opened it and threw the picnic tumbler outside.

Next out of the bag were the makings for a spliff. Chuck sat on the floor beside Alex and rolled the joint. He took a few drags himself before holding it out towards Alex's mouth. Alex shook his head, keeping his lips firmly closed.

'It's not optional,' Chuck said as he knelt closer to Alex. 'Open wide.'

Again, Alex shook his head but Chuck was behind him in a flash. With Chuck's hand covering his nose and most of his mouth, Alex eventually had to breathe in. Taking as shallow a breath as possible, he felt the smoke fill his mouth.

'One more for luck,' Chuck said, holding Alex's head tight, his nose closed, until Alex was forced to take in another breath.

Still groggy from whatever it was Chuck had used to knock him out, Alex felt his senses succumbing to the combined effects of the alcohol and the weed. He didn't trust what he saw next. Chuck took a round cake and his hunting knife from the plastic bag. The cake had coloured candles on top. A birthday cake.

'Time for the candles,' Chuck said, lighting them with his flint lighter. 'It's all right. Daniel's already had his piece. And his share of the vodka.'

Making a pantomime of taking a huge breath, Chuck then blew out all the candles. Little specks of coloured wax flew through the air.

'Make a wish, Daniel,' Chuck called. He cut a slice of cake and carried it over to Alex, spilling crumbs across the floor.

Alex opened his mouth voluntarily this time. The icing stuck to his teeth. Chuck gave him another slug of vodka out of the bottle to wash it down.

'Every good party ends in a drunken brawl, doesn't it?' Chuck said as he punched the side of Alex's face, then his stomach. He landed a kick in Alex's groin and Alex rolled onto the floor, yelling in pain.

Chuck picked up the rag doll Alex had dropped in the doorway. He held it in one hand, moving it around like a ventriloquist's dummy, letting it 'speak' his words. 'Now,' he said in a high-pitched singsong voice, 'What might you and Daniel be arguing about? Good friends that you are.' He waggled the doll from side to side. 'Could it be that Daniel was fed up with you being always on his back, checking his every move?' Chuck cocked the doll's head to one side as if it was waiting for an answer. 'Or that you would never take his advice? That could be it, couldn't it?'

Chuck was a blur. A blur that kept talking. Chuck relit the spliff. He dragged it down and closed his eyes as he breathed out.

'Or maybe he showed you this.' Chuck pulled out a mobile from his pocket and bent down to show the screen to Alex. It was the picture of Alex with glistening muscles, wearing the black curly wig and the black leather bootlace. The picture Angus had received on *his* phone.

So Chuck had sent it.

The doll sprang into action again. 'You wouldn't want Daniel knowing about your sordid means of making money, would you? You boys and your secrets, heh? What *are* you like?' Chuck said, using the singsong voice again.

Chuck ground the remains of the spliff on the face of the rag doll before letting them both drop to the floor. 'Or, then again, maybe it was because Daniel found out that you'd killed his sister.'

Alex lifted his head from the floor and fought to get himself onto his knees. Daniel didn't have a sister. Chuck was obviously off his head. He should have known Chuck was crazy right from the start.

'Ha. You thought you knew everything about him, didn't you? You two being friends since forever.'

It couldn't be true, but the look on Chuck's face made him keep listening.

'So ... let's consider why Daniel didn't tell you about Ellie, his long-lost twin sister. Might it have been because he wanted to keep something private? Something that you wouldn't meddle in.' Chuck glared at him. 'His sister ... a poor wee lass ... that you lent your jumper to before you killed her.'

Alex rolled his shoulders, shook his head, tried to clear his thoughts. A dead girl ... wearing his jumper?

'Of course, you didn't know that Daniel has a half-brother too, did you? More secrets, heh?' Chuck took a bite of the birthday cake. 'Although, to be fair, Daniel wasn't aware that the good-for-nothing father he's never known is my dad too.' He drained the dregs from the vodka bottle and threw it over his shoulder, letting it smash against the tiled fireplace.

'Do you know how old I am, Alex?'

Alex shook his head.

Chuck grabbed Alex's chin. 'Have a guess.'

Alex forced out his reply. 'Eighteen? Nineteen?'

'Eighteen in two months' time.'

Alex shrugged.

'Ten months older than Daniel.' Chuck held up his hands in front of Alex's face and wriggled all his fingers. 'Making me just a wee bitty baby when my lousy father was out impregnating some whore with twins.'

Alex tucked his toes on the floor beneath him. If only he could get to his feet.

'Not that anybody would have known a thing about it,' Chuck went on, 'if Little Miss Interfering Ellie hadn't thought she could worm her way into our lives.'

Chuck moved around the room, lighting the candles— their flames spitting and spluttering until they reached a steady glow.

'But she wouldn't listen, would she? Kept pestering to see Dad ... Saying all she wanted was to get to know him. Get to know my mum. MY mum. Well ... that couldn't happen, could it?'

Chuck glanced out of the window. 'We're the same you and me, Alex, aren't we? We know how to protect our mothers.' Then he swung the rucksack over his shoulders and picked up the hunter's knife from the table.

'Nearly over now, Alex,' he said lifting a candle from the floor and holding it close to his chin, making his features contort—like Alex and Daniel had done with torch beams on Hallowe'en when they were kids.

Chuck set down the candle 'How brave are you feeling, Alex?' He pushed the point of the knife into the skin below Alex's chin. 'Ready for the next challenge?'

Alex tipped his head back as Chuck pushed the point of the blade further home. A stream of warm liquid trickled down his neck.

'After tonight there'll be no more interfering bastards. And mum will be none the wiser.'

The realisation of what Chuck was admitting to hit Alex like a slap in the face.

'Are you ready, Alex, to go the same way as your bestie?'

'Where is he?'

'Ha ha. You think you are, don't you?' Chuck took the knife away from Alex's neck and used it to cut a length off a roll of gaffer tape. 'That's enough talking from you.'

When Alex's mouth had been taped shut, Chuck slid an arm around Alex's neck and hauled him backwards to the door. Propped against the doorframe, he watched as Chuck pushed the burning candle in the window seat against the heavy curtains. On his way out of the room, Chuck gave the trestle table a casual shove and the remains of the birthday cake flopped to the floor.

Chuck hoisted Alex to his feet and, shoving him along, they lurched out of the old office together as the flames that had taken hold of the musty curtains began to light up the room.

* * *

Angus came downstairs in a hurry. 'What is it?' he asked. 'I'm on my way out.' He unhooked his helmet from a coat rail and ushered Caitlin along the hallway and out on to the garden path.

Caitlin didn't want him to know she'd watched him arrive at the croft with Alex but there was no way around it. 'You were at Alex's.' She'd got his attention now. She continued as he studied her carefully. 'Look. It might be important. Did you take him somewhere?'

Angus' eyes narrowed. 'What do you know?'

'I don't really know anything.' And she didn't, so she might as well go for it. 'But I think he's in trouble.'

Angus nodded. He stepped back into the house and when he came out he was holding two helmets. 'Come on then.'

'Where're we going?'

'Dad just mentioned Jace had his van nicked today.'

Caitlin dangled the helmet by her side. 'And?'

'When I came away from the church ... after dropping Alex off there ... I think there was a white van parked on the drive behind the Manse.'

'Did Jace report it to the police?'

Angus shook his head. 'He thought maybe a mate had borrowed it. But nobody has.'

'You mean the Old Manse. Is that where you're going?'

Angus nodded. 'Are you coming, or what?'

Caitlin took the hint, put on the helmet and climbed up behind Angus.

CHAPTER 41

Snakes of smoke were already curling along the corridor when they reached the top of the stairs. With a push from Chuck, Alex toppled forwards. He tucked his head down for protection, unable to put out a hand as he bounced off the banister.

Chuck hurried down the stairs after him. He grabbed the back of Alex's jacket and half-dragged, half-pushed him through the kitchen and out of the back door.

There was a boom, then a roar, then a crack of breaking glass as a window blew out. Alex stumbled along the sloping garden path. The bindings above his knees were cutting painfully into his legs and he could only take tiny steps but he was eager to get away from the burning building even without the aid of Chuck keeping him upright and shoving him along.

Stumbling along like a couple of mutually supportive drunks, they reached a white van parked on the overgrown back drive.

Chuck opened the passenger door and hustled Alex in. Alex managed to caterpillar himself along the front seat before Chuck slammed the door.

Climbing into the driver's seat, Chuck fiddled with some loose wires and the engine rattled to life. With his hands still tied behind his back, Alex lurched around the cab as Chuck drove the van away from the burning Old Manse. And when Chuck slammed on the brakes, just before they reached the lochan, the van skewed to a halt across the track.

Chuck jumped out and Alex saw him disappear around the back of the van. He heard the rear door open and then a thumping as the van rocked from side to side.

A moment later Alex had his worst fears confirmed. Daniel, bent over double, his hands tied behind him, was being dragged along by Chuck.

Daniel obviously wasn't aware of him in the front of the van and although Alex tried to call out he made nothing more than a strangulated mewling against the tape covering his mouth.

Alex had to get out. He sidled along the seat to reach the door handle.

Then he saw it—on the floor of the cab—the flint lighter. It must have dropped out of Chuck's pocket.

He would have preferred Chuck's hunting knife. Even his own penknife that Chuck had scoffed at would have done the job. But the lighter would do. He slid off the seat, got in to a squatting position on the floor and, with his wrists still tied behind him, he scrabbled blind until he managed to get the lighter in his grasp.

With a tight hold on his quarry, he got himself back up on the seat and glanced through the windscreen. Chuck had already dragged Daniel into the lochan and was pushing him under the water. He could tell Daniel had no strength to fight back.

Alex realised, now, what Chuck had got planned. The stage-managed fallacious birthday party and Alex's supposed fight with Daniel. When both he and Daniel were found dead in the lochan, with the vodka, birthday cake and weed in their systems, the natural conclusion would be that their celebrations had ended with a fight in the water. And Alex would be implicated in the deaths of both Daniel and Ellie. Whether Chuck had intended this scenario all along or whether he'd seen an opportunity and taken it, Alex didn't know. What *was* clear to him though was that Chuck had been driven to all this to protect his mother from the truth.

It wasn't easy to flick the wheel of the lighter with his hands bound behind his back, but eventually he felt a flame burning in his cupped hands. Without being able to see what he was doing, positioning the lighter with his fingertips so that the flame was directed on the rope but without burning his flesh was impossible. And as the rope melted, the molten nylon burned into his skin too. Alex clenched his teeth against the pain. But as he kept stretching his wrists apart, he felt the rope weaken.

He dropped the lighter and swivelled to one side. Bringing his arms upwards in a fast-moving arc, he smashed his wrists and the rope against the steering wheel. The rope frayed enough for him to pull first one, then the other hand free.

He peeled the tape from his mouth, fumbled with the knots until he'd untied the rope biting in to his thighs, threw open the van door and ran, stumbling and yelling, to the lochan.

It was the smell that hit Caitlin first and as she peered around Angus' shoulder from her seat behind him on his scooter she saw black smoke swirling away from the hillside into the evening sky.

'Hurry up,' she called, but she knew Angus was going as fast as he could.

As they swung around the bends, getting nearer to the church and the Old Manse, the glow from the flames came into view.

They both jumped off the scooter when Angus parked up beside the church. Flames darting from the upstairs windows of the Old Manse lit up the graveyard and surroundings.

'I've no phone,' Caitlin yelled against the thundering roar.

Angus took out his and she watched him dial 999. Satisfied that was being taken care of, she rushed towards the Old Manse but came to a sudden halt when a hand grabbed the back of her jumper.

'Idiot. What're you up to?' Angus held her roughly.

'He's in there. I know.'

With his phone still clamped to the side of his face, Angus shook his head. 'The van has gone.' He marched Caitlin back to the scooter and kept a firm hold of her until he'd answered all the questions put to him by the emergency services operator.

Angus pointed to the back driveway. 'It was there before. They've gone.'

Caitlin stared at the burning building then turned to look at Angus. 'Where?'

Angus didn't answer but mounted the scooter. He waited while Caitlin hauled herself on behind.

When they reached the back drive, Angus turned to Caitlin and pointed to the tyre tracks in the muddy gravel. She nodded her understanding and Angus drove off to follow them.

They came to a halt at the lochan to see two boys wrestling in the water.

Caitlin kicked off her shoes, ran along the crumbling wooden pier and jumped in. The water was cold but, to her surprise, her feet found the bottom, the water only just skimming her shoulders. Angus jumped in close behind her.

'Daniel,' Caitlin screeched when she bumped into the floundering body that was parting the broad-leaved water lilies. She grabbed his sweater and half swimming, half wading, she started to heave him towards the wooden pier.

With Chuck's powerful hands clamped on his shoulders, pushing him further and further down so that his upturned face was only just above water, Alex saw Caitlin jump in. Heard her banshee squeal.

And Angus was there beside her, helping her pull Daniel towards the pier.

Alex fought back with a renewed effort. He clasped his hands together underwater then thrust his arms up, forcing Chuck's arms apart. Taking the chance to twist out of Chuck's grasp, he dipped below the water and circled around him. As he emerged, coming up right behind Chuck, he gripped his hands around Chuck's throat. Taking a deep breath to summon a final burst of energy, he nutted the back of Chuck's head.

Chuck flopped forwards and, like one of Mum's rag dolls, his body went lifeless in Alex's hands.

Suspecting a feint, Alex placed his hands on Chuck's back. He pushed down hard until he couldn't see Chuck anymore.

CHAPTER 42

A sound distracted him. A voice somewhere—shouting.

His arms heavy, his legs weak, Alex lay back and let the water take his weight, his arms floating by his side.

Shouting. More of it. He heard his name.

Then Angus was in the water beside him, grabbing him by the shoulder. 'Are you all right?'

Alex couldn't speak. He just stared into Angus' face—his blue eyes.

'You get out. I'll find him.' Angus dipped his head under the water.

Alex let his feet find the slippery stones on the bottom of the lochan and felt the water stream down his face and neck.

A moment later Angus resurfaced. 'I can't see him. It's too dark.'

Alex shook his head. 'What?'

'The boy. You were fighting. I can't see him.'

Comprehension hit. He'd thrust Chuck to the silty bed of the lochan—never to be seen again.

Alex ducked under the water. He was a stronger swimmer than Angus and could spend longer under the water. He searched—his hands groping around the rocks and clinging weeds—until he found the heavy bulk that was Chuck's body. With both hands, he grasped the back of Chuck's t-shirt and heaved him to the surface.

Angus took Chuck's shoulders and together they dragged the dead weight out of the water and up the muddy bank.

'I don't know what to do,' Angus said.

But Alex did and he moved like an automaton checking first for a pulse before going in to mouth to mouth rescue breathing. After the first round he looked across to where Daniel was stretched out on the pier, with Caitlin bending over him.

'Daniel had better be all right,' he hissed, pumping down on Chuck's chest with the heels of his interlocked hands.

The booming fire, still raging despite the two arcs of water aimed at it, made a deafening soundscape to the out-of-sync flicker of blue lights and the emergency workers milling around. Wrapped in a blanket and waiting by the ambulance where Daniel lay shivering under several blankets, Alex watched the proceedings around him. Caitlin, her teeth chattering, was sitting on the ambulance step, scowling. Chuck, handcuffed to a police officer and still wearing the blue latex gloves, was vomiting next to the police van. He couldn't see Angus anywhere.

Reverend Macaulay hurried over from where he'd just parked his car and climbed in the ambulance. 'Thank God.

Thank God,' Alex heard him say as he leaned over Daniel and placed a protective hand on his forehead.

'We'll get you lot away now,' a paramedic said jumping down the step. She helped Caitlin into the ambulance and motioned for Alex to get in too.

* * *

With the blanket still draped around his shoulders, Alex tipped the plastic chair backwards and let his head rest on the wall behind him. Across the corridor a uniformed police office barred the door to one of the hospital observation rooms.

Constable Logan was walking down the corridor followed by Caitlin and her dad. 'I've got everything I need for tonight. Get some sleep and I'll call by tomorrow afternoon,' the constable was saying to Caitlin.

Constable Logan then turned her attention to Alex. 'I'll see you outside,' she said before walking towards the hospital exit.

A nurse approached him. 'You can go in for a minute now,' he said, leading Alex to a side ward.

Daniel was lying in the bed with his eyes closed, tubes trailing from his hands, his dad hovering by his side.

'I'm sorry—' Alex started.

'Thank you ever so much,' Reverend Macaulay said before Alex could say another word. He held out his hand but changed his mind and pulled Alex into a hug.

Roused by their voices, Daniel opened his eyes. He looked into Alex's face and gave him one slow nod.

They'd made a deal. Alex had insisted that Constable Logan wasn't to contact his mum. She'd capitulated on the understanding that she gave him a lift home. Alex opened the passenger door on the police van and Constable Logan turned down the radio.

'Now I know you don't want to worry your mum, but I had to promise that nurse in there that I'd see you safe home.'

Alex gave her a steely glare.

'And in my mind, being on your own in the croft isn't really the best option.' She gave him a winning smile. 'I'm sure my hubby wouldn't mind me bringing home a waif for the night...'

Alex scowled.

'But how about I phone your Aunty Joan? Your mum's likely in bed by now. And I'd not be accused of neglecting my duty.'

'Seems like you'll do whatever you want,' Alex said. 'But I'm waiting outside while you talk to her.' He got out of the van and closed the door while Constable Logan took out her mobile.

'Well. Apart from needing some convincing that you were the hero of the piece ...' Constable Logan said as she joined him outside the van.

Alex gave her a *welcome to my world* shrug.

'...she wants you at the chalet where she can keep an eye on you.'

'For—' he bit back the *fucksake*.

'Come on.' Constable Logan opened the driver's door. 'Let's both of us get this night over with.'

Alex banged his fist on the roof of the van but then opened the passenger door and got in.

***

She watched Alex tap on the chalet door.

That woman really is a dragon, Logan thought to herself when Alex's Aunty Joan appeared with her curlers in, opening the door just a crack as if it was none other than Satan she was welcoming in.

There was no wave from Alex as he shuffled into the chalet. Logan switched on the engine but turned off the fan heater and opened her window. Alex had left his sodden blanket on the passenger seat and his damp smell filled the cab. She put the van into reverse and completed the tight manoeuvre in the limited space next to Stewart's Nissan then headed down the hill. It would be quieter to get her paperwork sorted at the station here before going back to sit in on the questioning of their suspect.

At her desk, she slid forwards an A4 sheet of paper. Names, dates of birth and, against a few of the names, grainy photographs of girls recently reported missing in Scotland. She'd crossed off the first three. Next on the list was Ellie Jacobs, missing from her foster parents at Bridge of Earn. She would have been 17 today.

TUESDAY

CHAPTER 43

Alex woke with the sun on his face and the smell of Brut in his nostrils. An empty sleeping bag on the blow-up bed beside him told him Stewart was up already. A folded clean shirt was on the end of the bed. Alex put it on with his almost dry jeans and hoodie.

Aunty Joan was up too—making porridge in the kitchen. She dolloped a ladleful into a dish. 'You can take it through,' she said pushing the dish across the worktop towards Alex.

He picked it up and carried it to Moth's bedroom where his mum lay sleeping. He roused her gently.

'Good morning, you,' she said with a smile.

It seemed liked pacing alone around the games pitch was becoming his new lunchtime activity. He'd completed a couple of circuits when Angus came jogging out of the changing room block and joined him.

'How you feeling?'

'Never better,' Alex replied.

Angus continued to walk alongside him.

'So … is that all?' Alex said.

'Aye. Mostly. I didn't really expect to see you today.'

'Always unpredictable, me.'

'And your usual charming self.'

He gave Angus a look. 'Look, thanks and everything. Last night … But I don't need a nurse maid.'

'I'll keep that in mind.'

They'd almost completed a full circuit of the pitch and were approaching the changing rooms again when Angus put a hand on Alex's forearm and pulled him, ever so slightly, towards the door.

'What?'

'Just talk to me.'

Alex reckoned he owed him that and after a quick glance to check the other kids were all engrossed in their football he followed Angus in.

Angus was standing beside the games teacher's office. He tried the door, which wasn't locked, and went in. Alex felt his guts clench and went in too.

There was very little floor space with all the shinty sticks, nets of kit and empty water bottles spilling everywhere.

'Fucksake. Who dressed you this morning, boy?'

Alex got hold of the lopsided collar of his shirt where Angus was pointing. He knew something hadn't felt right all morning. He unzipped his hoodie and fumbled with the top mismatched button and buttonhole of the shirt Stewart had lent him. Then Angus' fingers were helping, undoing five buttons in the time it took Alex to do the one.

Alex kept a wary eye as Angus readjusted the two sides of the shirt until they matched and fastened the bottom button. Alex took a half step back and did up the rest.

'There, that's better.' Angus patted Alex on the chest then straightened the shirt collar at the back of Alex's neck. 'So the gossip doing the rounds is that lad's some sort of psycho.'

Alex screwed up his eyes and nodded.

'Sorry. You can just tell me to shut up.'

'No. It's all right.' Alex took a seat on the teacher's swively chair. 'You, more than anybody, deserve to know.'

Angus sat on the edge of the desk and stretched out his legs.

'Turns out that psycho, as you rightly call him, killed Daniel's twin sister. And no, before you ask, I didn't know he had one either.'

'The girl on the beach.'

Alex nodded. 'He trapped her in the ice cellar at the Old Manse and when she was too weak to know what was happening, he drowned her. Leaving her to wash up a few days later.' He didn't mention what he'd overheard Constable Logan discussing with a colleague. How Chuck had used his skills with his hunting knife to make Ellie's face that bit more difficult to identify.

'So, you and him—?'

'Did some stupid things. Yes.' Alex gazed up at the polystyrene ceiling tiles, surprised to discover it was a relief to talk. 'I don't know … He was so sure of himself. The way he held his body, his'—Alex searched for a word to describe what he meant— *'rightness*. He would never expect to come second, or not succeed.'

'Narcissistic?' Angus looked serious; he wasn't showing off. He'd gone through his own mental process and had nailed it. And here he was, asking for Alex's confirmation that it was correct.

With that one word, spoken by Angus with such attention, Alex felt a tectonic plate shift under his world. He took a deep breath. Here was somebody who wanted to listen to him, somebody who understood.

He nodded. 'Yes, Chuck loved himself and expected everybody in the world to feel the same. In his twisted brain he was doing what was right—protecting his mum from a truth he knew would destroy her.'

'So Daniel—'

'Yep. Same plan. Except he used *me* to get to Daniel.' Alex thumped his fist on the desk. 'If only I'd never asked Daniel along.'

'Hey. He'd have found a way.'

'He even broke in our house, hacked my computer. It's not good knowing you've been manipulated.'

Angus put his hand over Alex's fist which was still scrunched up tight on the desk but Alex pulled it away fast, as if he'd been scalded.

'So, if that's all...' Alex said, standing up.

'Yeah. Sure.'

'And thanks for ... well...'

Angus nodded as he held open the door to let Alex walk back to the games pitch alone.

Getting home after school, Alex stopped short as he entered the kitchen. He hadn't been back since he'd left with Angus yesterday to go to the Old Manse. Mum's favourite mug still lay on the floor. He picked it up and set in upright on the kitchen table, placing the broken-off handle beside it. There was a knock at the door. Looking around at the mess, he blushed when Moth sidled in.

'Thought I'd come and … you know…' Moth eased past Alex and took the dustpan and brush out of the cupboard beneath the sink. She set to, clearing up the shards of broken crockery that littered the worktop and floor. 'Mum's getting quite teary at Aunty Cath leaving us.'

'We're hardly the other side of the universe. Mum would be pleased if she visited now and then.'

'Stranger things do happen I suppose. But you know how busy she is with the salon.'

'Hmm,' Alex said.

Moth had run water in the sink and was now using a cloth to clean around the worktop.

'I'll do that.' Alex took the cloth off her. 'You can collect the eggs.' He passed her a small wicker basket.

'Righty-ho.'

Alex sat at the table and put his head in his hands.

When Moth came back, she placed the egg basket on the worktop then picked up the broken mug and filled it with water. She held it up to the light coming in from the kitchen window.

'No leaks,' she said. 'You can't trust a glued-back-on handle for your cup of tea but it will be fine as a vase.' She took a posy of flowers from the wicker basket, dropped it in the mug, got a coaster from the cutlery drawer and set it on the table.

'Thank you,' Alex said.

Moth slipped a slender hand along the back of his neck. 'I'm sorry. I should have been there for you.'

Alex put his arm around her waist and pulled her towards him. 'Don't be stupid,' he said. 'I've not been the easiest person to be near lately.'

Moth rubbed her hand over the top of Alex's head and gave him a kiss on the cheek.

Alex ran his fingers under his collar as he felt his neck redden. 'Moth. You know ... you and me—'

'Are good friends?'

'Of course we are. It's just—'

'In your dreams, little cuz,' she said and he wasn't sure why she added a wink when she said, 'Don't worry. I know exactly what you mean.'

Alex was grateful for the rumble of tyres on the cattle grid.

'That'll be Stewart. I got him to drop me on the road before he went to the shop.' Moth picked up her bag. 'He'll bring Aunty Cath back after tea.'

'I know. And ... thanks.'

WEDNESDAY

CHAPTER 44

Alex hadn't seen him in school all morning. And it wasn't until he was silently working at a computer station, getting his head around the latest CAD assignment like the rest of the class, that he recognised his aftershave. From the corner of his eye, Alex watched Angus settle in a workspace further down the room. There were no requests for help, no communication about the tasks. And when Angus slipped out before the class ended without even having made eye contact, Alex wondered if he was being avoided.

'Hey, Angus,' Alex called as he hurried out of the workshop.

Angus turned back. 'Hi,' he said as Alex caught up with him.

'I was wondering if...?'

Angus stood looking at him, waiting. Kids pushed past them on their way to lunch.

'I wondered if you're vegetarian.'

Angus laughed. 'And you want to know, why?'

'I'm practicing my showstopper starter tonight. So I wondered if you would...'

'If I would…?'

'…like to come to tea?'

Angus turned away and when he turned back his face was straight, his eyes serious. 'I'd love to come to tea…'

'But?'

'Look I'm sorry if I got things wrong. But with that photo and things. It's just … I don't want to mess anybody about.'

Alex's face dropped. He had no reply ready for that and Angus walked away towards the common room.

Alex was regretting he'd planned such a complicated starter. There was a lot of last-minute cooking with sautéing the razor shells and deep frying the beetroot chips, yet he couldn't change it now.

His hands were shaking as he sliced the chanterelles he'd collected this morning.

Mum came in to the kitchen and began setting the table, laying out the cutlery and glasses of water.

'I don't know but … I think we'll need another place tonight,' Alex said. His stomach churning at not knowing whether he'd come or not.

'I thought Daniel was staying home until tomorrow.'

'He is. I'll go round after tea to see him. It's Angus.'

'Angus from the village? That's nice,' Mum said, setting out the extra place, just as Angus knocked on the back door.

'I'll bring you a coffee,' Alex called to Mum after they'd finished eating and she'd gone through to the living room.

'I'll just see to the hens, then you can add a biscuit to that,' she called back.

The starter had turned out all right, although the chanterelles, while they added the touch of autumn colour he'd aimed for, hadn't really worked flavour wise. The only outward injury he'd suffered throughout the proceedings was a burn on his wrist as he'd caught it on the side of the fryer. But on the inside … Angus had been charming to Mum, raving about the soup she'd made to follow his starter, but he'd hardly said anything directly to Alex.

Angus collected the dishes and carried them to the sink.

'Thanks for coming,' Alex said eventually to Angus' back. There was no reply.

Alex closed the small distance between them in preparation for the huge step he was about to take. He reached out and put a hand on Angus' shoulder. Angus turned around, soapsuds dripping from his fingers.

Alex was taken aback by the look on Angus' face.

'I need to be honest with you,' Angus said and Alex felt his mouth go dry. 'It's probably best for us not to hang out together.'

Alex frowned. This was so, so difficult. 'But I thought … we were all … okay?'

Angus shrugged. 'I suspect we might be okay in different ways. That I might want something you don't want.' Angus turned back to the sink, stacking the dishes in the drainer.

When he'd finished, he wiped his hands on a dish towel and picked up his helmet that he'd left on the worktop.

'No. Don't go.' Alex sounded desperate, he knew it. 'I *do* know what I want.'

Angus lifted his eyebrows to say 'really?'

'And I don't want to mess you about. It's just ...'

'Look. It's not been easy for me either,' Angus said, putting down his helmet again. 'But at some point, you just have to face up to being gay.'

He'd said the word. Alex wanted him to unsay it. Or did he?

'It can be a big deal, or mean nothing. It's the whole world, or nobody gives a shit. But unless you own it, you'll never know.'

They stood in silence for a moment. Then Alex asked, quietly, 'Do your parents know?'

'Not that I'm aware. I don't think they would even consider it a possibility. My dad's a road worker, my granddad was a road worker. The closest anyone in our family comes remotely to anything this way is when Dad's cousin Trevor puts two balloons up the front of his jumper at Hogmanay.'

Alex laughed at the image. 'And I've not got it wrong? You do like me?'

'What! I thought that was obvious.'

Was it? 'It's just...'

'What now?'

Alex got that Angus wasn't annoyed with him, he'd spoken more like a patient teacher. He felt able to say what was bothering him. 'Well … you're so much a ten … and I'm barely a five.'

Moving to stand beside him, Angus took hold of Alex's hand, interlocking their fingers. 'You run your own business, cook like a wizard, save goals as if you could do it in your sleep…' Angus gave him a brief appraising glance. 'And with pecs like that—no way are you a five.'

Alex turned so that they were face to face. He took hold of Angus' other hand. Their kiss this time was long and hard and Alex wanted it never to stop.

* * *

The curtains at the minister's study were drawn closed Alex noticed as he walked around to the back of the Manse. He gave a tentative knock on the door and when Eva eventually opened it, she pulled him into a huge hug, burying her face in his shoulder.

'He's upstairs,' she said with a grim expression when she released him. 'See what you can do with him.'

Alex sprinted up the two flights of stairs. He understood the reason for Eva's words when he pushed open Daniel's bedroom door and saw the scowl on Daniel's face. He was lying on his bed, headphones on, wearing a t-shirt and boxer shorts with the whole of his lower right leg wrapped in bandages.

Alex sat on the desk chair and pushed aside a plate of unfinished scrambled egg and toast.

'It looks a lot worse than it is,' Daniel said, taking off his headphones and lifting his bandaged leg in the air. 'I think the nurse wanted to make a point.'

'Maybe she thought it needed protection.'

'Don't you think I get enough of that.'

Fair point, Alex thought, but he wasn't going to get trapped in that conversation.

'Here. I brought you this.' Alex tossed a cardboard tube onto the bed by Daniel's hand. 'Mum wanted to send you lavender bags to help you sleep but I persuaded her to get you this.'

Without a word, Daniel removed the plastic lid and slid out the poster. He unrolled it and nodded his appreciation at the glossy picture of AC/DC.

'Top drawer,' Daniel said, pointing at his desk.

Alex opened the drawer and took out the packet of Blu Tack Daniel wanted.

With a bit of tricky manoeuvring Daniel kneeled on the bed and stuck the poster on the wall.

'That's better. Just like the old days,' Alex said when Daniel was satisfied the poster was up right. 'Hey, don't glare at me,' he added when Daniel turned back to face him. 'I'm one of the good guys, remember.'

But Daniel's expression merely changed from a scowl to a frown. 'How could he do it?' he said at last.

Alex shook his head. His own face reflecting Daniel's anguish.

'And do you know where my father is ... right now?'

Alex shook his head again.

'Visiting the bastard.'

Alex wheeled the desk chair closer to the bed.

'And Eva just backs him up.' Daniel's voice came out thick. 'Telling me it's what he has to do. It's his *job*.'

Alex stretched out and took Daniel's hand. He held it tight as Daniel squeezed his eyes shut and tears streamed down his cheeks.

THURSDAY

CHAPTER 45

Daylight had barely tinged the sky with a pink glow when Alex rolled out of bed. Down in the kitchen he started to prepare Mum's porridge; then, keeping as quiet as possible so as not to disturb her, he set up the ironing board.

'Here. I can do that,' Mum said as she came up softly behind him.

'It's this stupid collar,' Alex said, twisting the shirt about on the ironing board.

'I know. Let me show you.'

When his clothes were as crease free as possible, he draped them over his arm and sprinted upstairs to shower and shave.

The mirror in his bedroom was small but as he was putting his PE kit and his copy of *The View From the Bridge* that they'd started reading in English yesterday in his backpack he caught sight of himself. Not too shabby, he decided, running a hand over his hair.

'See you later,' he said to Mum as he looked in on her in the kitchen. She still had shadows beneath her eyes but she'd insisted he wasn't to make a fuss. 'I'll make bean casserole for tea,' he added as she waved him off.

He was in plenty of time to wait on the road for Daniel but he needed to make a detour to the clifftops first. There was a lot he had to discuss with Dad.

A constant stream of kids passed Alex as he waited. He checked the time: 8:50. Had Daniel changed his mind about coming to school today and Alex hadn't got the message? Five more minutes, then he'd have to go. The main course of his showstopper would take the whole double lesson of hospitality this morning; he needed to be on time.

When he saw Daniel limping up the road he understood. Daniel must have won the argument about not needing a lift and they continued up the hill together.

As they turned on to the road to school Alex heard the familiar rattly sound of Angus' scooter approaching, and then slowing to a stop beside them. Angus balanced one foot on the curb and took a polybag of white powder from his jacket pocket. He passed it to Alex.

A bunch of kids on bikes turned the corner. 'Alex and Daniel up a tree. K.I.S.S.I.N.G,' they chanted as they passed by.

Daniel looked uncomfortable at the homophobic taunt but Alex glanced at Angus and almost smiled.

'Thanks,' Alex called as Angus gave a wave and rode off again.

'Arrowroot,' Alex said holding up the polybag. 'They didn't have any in the shop and I need some this morning. Angus' mum had some.'

'Just because he helped save my life doesn't mean I have to like him,' Daniel said, stomping on ahead while Alex dropped the arrowroot into his backpack.

Daniel's wasn't the only life that had been saved by Angus that night, Alex knew. It had never been mentioned by any of them, but last night Alex had had nightmares about Chuck's rotting dead body surfacing on the lochan. He knew that could easily have been a consequence if Angus hadn't been there.

'Caitlin will be glad to see you back at school,' Alex said, catching up with Daniel and, on cue, Caitlin darted out of the school doorway to meet them.

'Caitlin's coming round after school,' Daniel said, turning to Alex. 'To help me catch up.'

'No problem,' Alex said.

'But you'll come after tea?'

Alex nodded. 'I've got some English notes for you too.'

He watched Daniel and Caitlin file into the science wing then waved to the school secretary as he passed her office. With the bell ringing to start the school day, Alex took the stairs two at a time to the Hospitality room.

ALSO AVAILABLE FROM STONE COLD FOX PRESS

Aphra's Child
LESLEY GLAISTER

ISBN: 978-0-9926514-7-3
Format: Paperback
Size: B Format (198 x 129 mm)
Extent: 382 pp

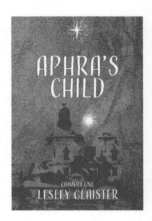

Tula is a chimera, a girl with a tail. She's been raised secretly in a remote highland glen by her mother and protector, Aphra. But one day Aphra is taken and, all alone, Tula is forced to fend for herself. She finds her way to the city, a hostile and dangerous place for any chimera especially one as naïve as Tula.

Will she find the help she needs and the answers she craves before her secret is discovered?

'This is a thoroughly enjoyable young adult debut, but with more substance than most. I really had a hard time putting this down, it was utterly immersive.'

—Lou, Top 100 reviewer on Amazon

'Oh this was so good! Complex character development and world building...'

—Brigette Wade, review on Netgalley

www.stirlingpublishing.co.uk